# The Spellbrook

JD Cooper

Other books by the author

*A Cup of Tea with Mr Johnstone*

*Dorcas The Invisible Cleaner*

*The Orb of Alberston*

*Eddie's Diner*

*The Miracle of Siterni*

*Jack's Shadow*

Copyright © 2023 J D Cooper. All rights reserved. No portion of this book maybe reproduced in any form without permission from the publisher, except as permitted by U.K. copyright law. For permissions contact: jdcooper999@hotmail.com

*Our very eyes
Are sometimes, like our judgments,
blind.*

*William Shakespeare*

# Table of contents

| | |
|---|---|
| Prologue | 1 |
| Chapter One | 5 |
| Chapter Two | 9 |
| Chapter Three | 18 |
| Chapter Four | 25 |
| Chapter Five | 32 |
| Chapter Six | 39 |
| Chapter Seven | 46 |
| Chapter Eight | 54 |
| Chapter Nine | 57 |
| Chapter Ten | 64 |
| Chapter Eleven | 70 |
| Chapter Twelve | 77 |
| Chapter Thirteen | 89 |
| Chapter Fourteen | 95 |
| Chapter Fifteen | 101 |
| Chapter Sixteen | 106 |
| Chapter Seventeen | 114 |
| Chapter Eighteen | 119 |
| Chapter Nineteen | 127 |
| Chapter Twenty | 135 |
| Chapter Twenty-One | 141 |
| Chapter Twenty-Two | 146 |
| Chapter Twenty-Three | 151 |
| Chapter Twenty-Four | 157 |

| | |
|---|---|
| Chapter Twenty-Five | 161 |
| Chapter Twenty-Six | 167 |
| Chapter Twenty-Seven | 171 |
| Chapter Twenty-Eight | 176 |
| Chapter Twenty-Nine | 182 |
| Chapter Thirty | 186 |
| Chapter Thirty-One | 194 |
| Chapter Thirty-Two | 197 |
| Chapter Thirty-Three | 209 |
| Chapter Thirty-Four | 214 |
| Epilogue | 222 |

# The Spellbrook

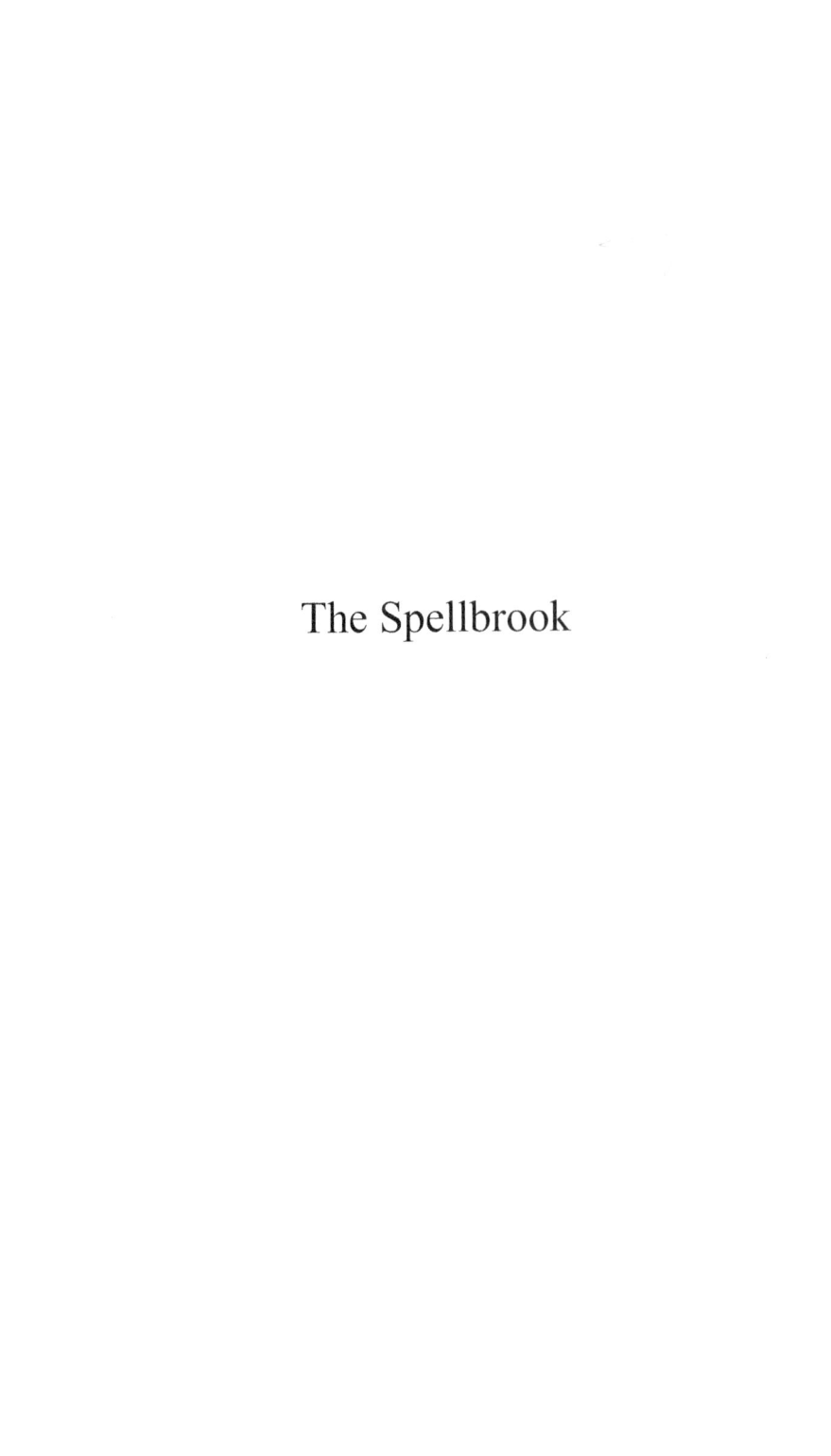

## *Prologue*

As the hammer came down for the seventh, or was it the eighth time on the recumbent man's head, the holder of the oh so blunt instrument wondered, could anyone really justify such violence? Such brutality? Were so many blows really necessary to accomplish the objective? Probably not they thought, maybe one or two really well-placed ones to the head would have done the job, but let's say someone entered your house, unannounced and uninvited in the early hours of the morning, savagely slayed the woman you say you loved as she lay sleeping the sleep of the righteous, then, well, a person could easily panic couldn't they? Get caught up in the moment, overreact possibly?

Imagine waking up, struggling to breathe and thinking you'd wet yourself, which let's face it would be bad enough in the early hours of the morning, but only to actually find that your wife was lying there with her throat slashed wide open and someone was sitting astride you with an enormous knife in their hand about to do the same thing to you.

No, they were sure that the police would understand the situation and see things from the householder's point of view - a person defending their castle and so on. The intruder was lucky they were no longer in America though - they'd probably have faced the wrong end of a .45 calibre or worse in some trailer park type settings - a shotgun or a hunting rifle perhaps, who knew?

Then again why would someone want to break into a trailer, what would there be worth stealing in what was essentially a caravan on bricks, and anyway this wasn't America, this was leafy suburban Surrey, and intruders were ten a penny in this particular part of the country; the police would probably have a quick look around, put it down to an occupational hazard on the part of the intruder and move on. One less maniac to warn people about, one less obviously extremely violent and bloodthirsty individual to anticipate coming across in a dark alleyway somewhere when you're walking the streets at night on your own. No, the world was better off without intruders of that sort thank you very much, I think we'd all agree.

And if only that's what had happened, we could have all merrily sailed off into the sunset, we could have all gone on our way, thinking natural justice had somehow occurred. The householder would have been hailed a hero for stemming, or at least slowing the tide of throwaway violence, the sort of stuff that's in the news one day and forgotten the next.

The dead wife would have been incorrectly remembered at her funeral as a wonderful woman, full of charm and grace, and such a loss, such a loss. And the dead intruder would have been shown to be the violent psychopath they so obviously always were and never spoken of, or thought about again.

And if only that was what had happened, but it wasn't.

However, I *can* explain. I'm not a bad person, really I'm not, and, if an Englishman defending his castle had you readily agreeing that they could justify smashing the brains out of some poor intruder, rather than just knocking them unconscious before calling His Majesty's finest; then surely you'd give me the chance to explain things from my point of view.

You'd have to know the full story though; you'd have to understand everything that I'd been through to bring me to that position - that position being sitting astride an elderly householder lying in his king-sized bed whilst I was holding a lump hammer in one hand and a really sharp knife in the other. I know, it sounds quite bad doesn't it but let me try and explain?

## *Chapter One*

Thomas - 1900

I suppose any story should have a beginning, a middle and an end, but I'm sure you don't want to hear about someone's troubled childhood, someone's lack of education and someone's poor upbringing - better I think that I start at the mid to end part - that's probably best, probably most convenient for all concerned, and in any event I didn't have any of those things that people think you have to have had to make a good story; and without which they would say, it left no story at all.

If the point of *my* story though is to explain how someone like me can do what I did and think they were justified, and consider themselves to be a good person throughout, then I better start off by saying that I'd done no harm to anyone, up until that point, being a doctor that sort of went with the job. 'Primum non nocere' - 'First, do no harm' was what we were told to live by when we signed on to be doctors. It comes from Hippocrates - the original doctor and the man who is believed by many to be the father of medicine.

Whatever the truth is, and whoever actually said it, I've always tried to keep the oath uppermost in my mind and I'm proud to say that up until what happened, I'd never knowingly done harm to anyone, for whatever reason, in fact I have gone out of my way to uphold my beliefs and tried to treat people with as much love, care and attention as I could, regardless of who they are and where I found them.

I'd finished medical college and gone straight into surgery - that was all I ever wanted to be - a surgeon. Being a doctor was one thing but I wanted to do more, to be more. I wanted to save lives every day and in my early years I felt that saving the body - restoring it to its best form was the greatest service I could offer. The mind was for others - for those who wanted to talk people better, and I'm not saying there isn't a place for that - just that actually healing the body seemed a better way of treating someone and so for another eight years on top of my two years general training I studied, I worked non-stop and eventually qualified as a surgeon.

Throughout my training I had one true friend - Lawrence Jacobs. He had been my 'right-hand man' on many occasions, both at medical college and in my life, and he would have been my best man when I married Laura some years later, if he hadn't had to work at the last moment, but was a regular visitor to our house ever since.

We sometimes had weekends away with him and the children - Saul and Eloise, who loved him - 'Uncle Lawrence' seemed to be an almost semi-permanent fixture for a few years at our house until things started to unravel.

But I am racing ahead of myself, and I haven't even told you about Laura. During our training Lawrence and I were allowed to attend the Spellbrook Hospital as his father knew someone there, and it was through this happy circumstance that I met my future wife.

When I first saw her she was but a young woman and was attended to by a kindly nurse in the gardens. She was the most naturally beautiful thing I had ever seen and I knew I must make her mine. I didn't know at that stage why she was at the hospital and then, before I knew it she was gone. Though I asked after her no-one knew who she was or where she had gone.

When Lawrence and I returned however, two years later, and now as qualified doctors I was astounded to see Laura back at the hospital and knew that this must be fate, this was no chance meeting and I wasn't going to let her escape me a second time.

I made it my business to be in the gardens when she was but saw she must now be a married woman, as if I wasn't mistaken she was with child.

I don't think this sat too well with her as she no longer seemed the youthful vibrant woman I'd seen two years before, but almost worn down with the world. She wore no wedding ring and it made me wonder if she were perhaps widowed, which could have explained her being back at the Spellbrook, perhaps recuperating after her loss. I felt immediately that I must help her, that it was my duty as a gentleman to do so. I knew I wasn't being rational and was allowing myself to be beguiled by her beauty, but I imagined a life with her, caring for her and providing for her.

I tried to discuss this enchanting woman and my thoughts with Lawrence but he seemed strangely disinterested and told me I should focus on my career instead, saying that she was probably a mentally ill patient and that we should not mix with 'her sort'; but I couldn't get out her out of my mind and kept going back to the gardens in the hope of seeing her one more time.

## Chapter Two

1900 - Laura

I suppose I'd agree that any story should have a beginning, a middle and an end, and I will touch very briefly on my childhood, but just to tell you that whilst I also didn't have a troubled one, it wasn't perhaps as straightforward as it could have been.

And if the point of *my* story is to explain how someone like *me* can do what *I* did and think they were justified, and all the while consider themselves to be a good person throughout, then I better start off by saying that I'd also done no harm to anyone either, at least up until that point, though I was sorely tempted at times.

My first memory, when I was about five years old, was of my aunt Charlotte, a caring and attentive woman who loved me like a daughter - like a mother should. I loved her like a daughter did and I believed that she would live forever - every morning she was there for me, waking me, dressing me and feeding me. And every night she read to me and tucked me into bed, kissing me goodnight and telling me she would see me in the morning.

When I was ten she sat me down and told me I was old enough to be told the truth, that she wasn't my mother but that *she*, my real mother loved me very much, as did my father. I didn't care for this truth and didn't believe it.

I remember asking her why, if they loved me so much, had they sent me away as soon as I was born, and was told that at that time they couldn't cope, they couldn't give me what parents should give a child and so they felt they had to ask Charlotte to take care of me, and I suppose they were proved right, she did take care of me, like a mother should.

Charlotte lived for another five years after she told me the truth and in those five years we often talked about what would happen to me after she was gone. At first I cried, not wanting to talk about death at all let alone hers, the woman who I considered to be my mother. I couldn't imagine being without her, living in this great big house on my own, no-one to talk to or to practise my reading with. How could she talk so freely about it I asked her? But all she would say was that death was part of life and that I must not be afraid of it, but that I must embrace it.

Five years later Charlotte died and the house was left to me, a fifteen-year-old girl. Or rather the house was left to me with my real parents, people I'd never seen in my life, acting as my trustees until I turned twenty-five, like I was some tragic Victorian heroine.

The house was sealed and I was driven to the railway station by the local vicar, whom Charlotte had entrusted my travel arrangements to. Several hours later I was rudely awoken by a porter and told I needed to leave the train.

I remember sitting alone on the platform, with what little belongings I'd brought with me by my side in a small suitcase, and wondering, what happens now? Where do I go? Who will look after me now?

My questions were answered almost an hour later when a man and a woman sat next to me, on my bench, but they said nothing. Were these my parents? It was like they were studying me, was I acceptable to them, did I pass their examination? And there we sat for what seemed like an eternity until they stood and told me to follow them. And so that's how I met my parents' servants - my parents, my real parents couldn't even be bothered to come and collect me themselves and had sent their servants.

We travelled, again in silence and almost an hour later arrived at a grand house where I was shown to a room at the rear by the woman who told me that dinner would be served shortly. There was no appearance from my mother, my real mother, no welcoming embrace of any kind.

Following dinner, I remember being summoned and entering a large and imposing room at the front of the house where the woman servant told me to sit and wait.

A door opened and a man and woman entered the room, closely followed by a girl of perhaps twelve years old who sat when told to do so with her hands folded neatly on her lap and her head bowed; her attention averted from who turned out to be her big sister, though she never acknowledged me as such for the rest of her life.

The man and woman introduced themselves as Mr and Mrs Foreman and told me that that was how I was to refer to them in public and that I was to be referred to as 'cousin Laura'. They told me that things would be better if I continued to stay in one of the back bedrooms, omitting to say what they meant - one of the servant's bedrooms. And that was that, that was how I met my parents.

I'm sure you'd agree that what I've described to you could have had a damaging effect on the wrong sort of person, and whilst I don't think that I *was* the wrong sort of person, I felt I couldn't live with the Foremans - or Clara, anymore, and so I made things 'difficult' for them, I failed to conform to their rules, either in public or in private, and whilst I didn't hurt them physically they eventually felt it would be better if I was 'sent to America for my education' - this was when I wasn't yet sixteen, so imagine if you will, I'd previously and for all of my formative years lived with woman who loved me, and whilst she wasn't my mother she loved me like she was. I'd had my own room, and was free to roam the house and gardens at will. Compare this to being sent on a train and deposited on a station platform and collected, not by those who bore you and should have raised you, and loved you, but their servants and confined to a room, not allowed to wander happily in the garden, or visit the local village, or mix with other children - and although I try to fool myself, it did have an effect on me. The thing that had a tremendous effect on me though was the actual being sent away itself, by my mother and father, not for education as they had told me and also somewhat closer than America.

I'd been roused from my sleep during the night, taken by the man and woman who had brought me to the house and placed in a carriage with my things. Though I kept asking them, they wouldn't tell me where I was going and I believed I was indeed en route to America. The journey though was considerably shorter and I found myself, at its end, being taken roughly from the carriage by two men dressed in white and injected with something into my arm.

The following morning, I woke and found that I couldn't move, as I'd been strapped to a bed, its sheets white and crisp. The air was sickly sweet and the room was in almost complete darkness.

For a fifteen-year-old girl to be confined in such a place was unimaginable and I must confess that I didn't make it easy for the staff at the hospital. I tried to keep my thoughts and my fears to myself, and also hold onto the desperate hope that my mother and father would at least visit me soon, perhaps today, or tomorrow, but they didn't and it was hard for me to stay calm at times. Medication was often needed to subdue me and apparently I did often become quite violent.

I spent three years at the hospital - the Spellbrook, it was called - and only ever saw the world and the sunlight when one kindly nurse took me outside into the gardens, which she sometimes did if she had some spare time.

It was during one of these times in the brightly lit gardens that I first saw Thomas, who was walking with another man, whom I didn't know at the time.

I asked the nurse who the men were and she told me that they were student doctors at the hospital. They would have nothing to do with us though, she said, the people who were kept downstairs, out of sight of everyone. The nurse, whose name was Emily, told me that I wasn't like the others kept here and that she felt sure I'd soon be going home. It was something to focus on, she said, something to keep my spirits up for - but I felt that the fact that I'd be taken back by my 'mother and father' and allowed to live in a back room among the servants wasn't such a wonderful thing to look forward to.

Had I then known what the alternative was, I'd have willingly run barefoot all the way back to my bedroom with the servants and wept in the arms of Mr and Mrs Foreman, begging for their forgiveness; as a horror unimaginable for any woman let alone a young girl was to befall me, not just on one night but on many.

I will not go into details for they are not fit for print but within six months of being reclaimed by my parents I found that I was with child. I'd believed it was a dream - or rather a nightmare the first time, and said nothing to Emily or the other nurses, but then each time it happened, each time being the same man, the man I'd seen in the gardens, I knew it was neither a dream nor a nightmare, but the actions of a depraved individual.

Having been brought back to the world by my parents I tried to be the daughter they wished for, but they already had that in Clara and let me know that nearly every day - they didn't need another one.

I told them what had happened at the hospital, the hospital they had sent me to, but they didn't believe me and told me I was making it up.

I didn't make things easy for my parents but they wouldn't believe me or let me see my daughter, whom I'd called Eloise and so I was again returned to the Spellbrook for 'convalescence' this time, rather than education.

However, the ghastly experiences I'd encountered were to be repeated by the same man and less than a year after returning I was again pregnant.

The nurses, those who would listen to me, said they were powerless to do or say anything to aid me as no one would believe me and so I suffered once again at the hands of an animal masquerading as a man, and a doctor at that. But that was when I met Thomas and knew I had to find a way out of this situation for myself.

## *Chapter Three*

Thomas 1902

People will tell you all sorts of things when they think they need to, and looking back now I realise how easily I was taken in. I considered myself a decent man, one who trusted people and wanted to be trusted by them, but I didn't consider myself to be naive.

I'd wanted to believe in Laura, I'd wanted her to be the pure, youthful woman I'd first seen and so, when I saw her again and heard her tale, I knew I must do 'the right thing'. I'd wanted to be that noble man, that white knight, the one every man yearns to be at some stage in their life, and help this poor woman out of her terrible situation. Every man wants to do that at some point, to save a soul if only to make ourselves feel better.

She told me that her husband had died, and I believed her.

She told me that she had two children by this man, and I believed her.

She told me that she was convalescing following her husband's death and that she would shortly be returning to her house in the north of the country.

And when that was added to the first and second stories it was easy to believe as well. I wanted to believe her, and accepted the ready-made family she offered.

Within weeks of seeing her again at the Spellbrook I proposed to Laura and we were married a short time later in a small ceremony at my former church, with Eloise as a bridesmaid.

We had been so looking forward to our big event and I hoped that any differences that existed between Laura and her parents would be resolved from now on, or if not, at least put aside for the time being. I hoped that this day of celebration could herald a new beginning for Laura and her parents and that how they had treated her could be left where it belonged - in the distant past.

Lawrence was to be my best man but as I waited at the church until the last possible moment for him to arrive I started to doubt him and recalled how dismissive he had been of Laura when she was at the hospital. It was almost as if he wanted to be nowhere near her and wanted me to totally forget her, which I could not.

With only moments to go before the ceremony a telegram arrived for me telling me that Lawrence had had to work late and couldn't attend to perform his duties.

It was to sour our relationship in the future and I didn't see him as much as I used to. Things had changed between us and I wondered if there was perhaps a jealousy there? Was he envious of me finding the woman of my dreams?

And we were to be disappointed on all sides as Laura's parents also failed to attend though they sent no apology at all. We were later informed that one of Clara's children was sick and that they had travelled to her house to give her support.

This did nothing to help Laura's situation with her parents, or calm her, but she bore it well in front of the remaining small congregation, mainly made up from local people who I understood attended local weddings, almost as a day out. My own side was very small already, in that my parents had died a few years before and I was an only child.

We sold Laura's former home in the north of the country, which I never saw, and bought our own house nearer to London, so I could continue working at the hospital. Laura told me that she was a woman of means having inherited her husband's considerable wealth, and I took her at her word.

The children, Eloise and Saul were happy and had a good relationship with their grandparents, and that allowed Laura and I time to build our own, and get to know each other outside the confines of the hospital.

I realised quite quickly that Laura wasn't a well woman and was prone to bouts of melancholy, if not depression. These manifested themselves in Laura spending days in her bedroom and not speaking to anyone. We had no servants and so I brought her her meals, although she hardly ever ate them.

Laura's parents helped us as and when they could with the children, but whilst they were close to Eloise and Saul I sensed a vast distance between them and their daughter, and it seemed that they each acted a role in public, a facade, purely for show.

They put their non-attendance to our wedding to one side and though they explained the reason for it to Laura and expected her to accept it, they offered no apology at all, and never mentioned it to me.

I often asked Laura why she and her parents seemed so detached from each other, but all she would say is that it was complicated and that they had never been close, but that she would have to make the best of it and treat them accordingly.

She told me that they had sent her away when she was young, to better her education, but what I saw of Laura's education made me suspect it wasn't a boarding school they had sent her to, and perhaps she resented them for that, and that was why she wasn't as loving as a daughter should be, but even if that were the case I failed to see *their* excuse.

Laura's father was a taciturn man who often only spoke to welcome dinner being served or it being bedtime for the children, whereas her mother was quite happy to air her views on all manner of subjects.

However, when I'd tried to broach the subject of her strained relationship with Laura I found her mother strangely unwilling to spout forth, telling me instead that I should speak to my wife, but I often had difficulties doing even that if Laura was in the wrong sort of mood.

I'd taken up my position at the Spellbrook and was working the long hours expected of a junior doctor, but even so when I came home I wanted to be welcomed by my loving wife, as a husband should be, but often I found Laura's door locked and the light dimmed. We had been married nearly two years and whilst the months passed our closeness, our intimacy, came no nearer to being realised as I'd hoped it would once we were married.

Again, Laura fell silent on the subject and though it frustrated me I didn't feel it right to press her on the matter.

I can't recall exactly when it was that it crossed my mind, however briefly, that perhaps Laura saw ours as a marriage of convenience, and I hated myself for even fleetingly thinking such a thing.

She told me that she loved me, even if she didn't physically show it, and I believed her, why would she lie? But once I'd thought such a thing I couldn't rid it from my mind and it started to gnaw away at me and, if I am honest, at our relationship.

It was, I think at about the same time that Lawrence asked a favour of me. He clearly had a lavish lifestyle and was in his words 'a bit strapped at the moment' - a term he often repeated whenever he returned to work after a night out on the town, or a weekend away with his latest conquest - he was a debonair man, good looking some would say, and there seemed to be many of these conquests - if only according to Lawrence.

He asked if he could stay with us for a short time whilst he looked about for his own accommodation and whilst I was immediately happy to make space in our house for my lifelong friend, Laura wasn't so willing to oblige him and I had to be very firm on the subject, which caused heated rows between us and led to her staying with her mother for a short time. I couldn't understand the animosity Laura showed towards Lawrence and she would not explain it, perhaps there was a jealousy there, who could say?

And so it was that Lawrence moved in with us. We currently had a number of spare rooms and he took the back bedroom and as our shifts often overlapped each other's I barely saw him.

Lawrence had been with us for only a short time when I started to notice a change in Laura. She had become colder and harsher when we were alone, but even more so with our guest, almost to the point of rudeness and she would not explain herself when I asked her about it.

As things transpired Lawrence only stayed with us for a short while before he found lodgings on the other side of the city, although he did stay at our house from time to time, especially if he had had to work into the night, as he appeared to have to, perhaps more regularly than most.

## *Chapter Four*

The air of fractiousness continued between us for some weeks and I started to wonder if Laura may be in need of another period of 'rest'. She hadn't been herself for some time and although me working long hours didn't help, there was little I could do about it when I *was* at home. Laura seemed more agitated when Lawrence stayed with us, and I couldn't fathom why this would be. He was a friend and he loved the children, so I didn't see what the problem was and told her so.

I'd enquired at the hospital about what facilities were available for female recuperation but had been told there were none, and that it would not be appropriate for my wife to be a patient at the Spellbrook. Laura also point blank refused to voluntarily return to any form of hospital in any event.

We had many disagreements obviously, things usually started, like with many other couples our age in a new marriage, with a petty argument, well, not even that sometimes - a minor disagreement really, the origins of which I could never truly recall.

I'd say something, then she'd say something and before we knew it there were harsh words being thrown across the room, then objects, and then ultimately threats of mothers being stayed with - the usual things I suppose between strong willed people as we were.

Laura had stayed with her mother several times since we'd been married - but she always sent her back to me and maybe that was the problem, the finality of it all, the realisation that this was 'us', this was everything that we'd ever amount to, and things weren't going to change that much no matter how many times she 'took a break' or 'had a rest'. My wife was 'troubled' I think the modern term is, but at that time I didn't know how troubled she had been, nor still was.

I tried not to outright blame her for our arguments, certainly I never said the words 'it's your fault', but I perhaps wasn't as understanding as I should have been, and as it turned out I was so badly wrong about things - if only I'd known the truth then. Maybe then I'd have treated her better and saved us both from the future that awaited us.

The difficulties we were having made me reflect on what I actually knew of my wife - I'd first seen her at a hospital, but could find no record of her being there - had she been booked in under a false name, and if so what was it, and why?

Did it merely come back to her parents' social concerns - did they not want to be the parents of a mental patient, if that's what they considered her to be? I could not look at her in that way - she was my Laura, and always would be - I'd do everything I could for her - I'd die for her.

I knew so little of Laura's past, and then only what she told me. Her parents would not speak to me about their daughter, telling me to speak to her. They felt it wasn't for them to interfere in a marriage, and yet they continued to stay on and off with us, rent free and force themselves between us on a daily basis.

I'd accepted that Laura's first husband had died, leaving her with two children and yet she never spoke of him, there were no pictures of the man, and the silences from her parents on the subject gave me cause for concern as to who he had been.

I didn't want to lose Laura, I loved her, and I'm almost sure she still loved me. I just felt that she'd lied to me, and that made me wonder if she had been unfaithful to me - just in the way her arguments lost steam when we went down that road, pointing fingers at each other, and she never totally denied it. But even though I had no proof I'd vowed to forgive her if I found it to be true.

I no longer wondered who the other man had been, it didn't matter anymore, certainly not to me, and Laura had abruptly stopped her evening 'needlework classes', if such a thing actually existed and she'd ever gone to them, so I presumed she'd moved on as well. It was a difficult subject to discuss, there wasn't any proof, and she'd stayed with me anyhow, so I thought I should, in some way, be grateful.

Laura's parents weren't the sort of people you could really speak to, and it wasn't the done thing to air your problems to everyone else and so it built up and built up between us. Laura going to her mother and no doubt telling her it was all down to me and what a monster I was, and me? Well, I just bottled it up apparently, according to Laura. I 'internalised' it, in professional modern speak.

Having been at her mother's again, Laura came back and we were 'carrying on as best we could' but then, a few days later her parents arrived again, almost as if it were prearranged and they stayed with us to 'support her'. I felt that their presence made a difficult situation even harder, but we agreed we would try to make it work for the sake of the children, to make our family complete once more, and to give her a sense of focus.

Laura had apparently been at a number of hospitals in London, but she didn't have a career, and had never thought of going back to her old one whatever that had been, once she'd had the children. Also, with me being at work and putting in the hours I did, we were kept apart for long periods of the day. The children, we decided, should fill the void in our lives and occupy Laura when I wasn't at home. We couldn't afford nannies and she'd always said she wanted to try to raise the children herself, obviously with the help of her parents, and so we settled back into our married lives as best we could.

So, Laura's parents were currently staying with us, and this always caused friction between my wife and I. It wasn't the things that *were* said that caused issues for those currently around the dining table but rather the things that weren't. They were, in public at least, quite sociable, but I detested them for how they had treated Laura in the past and still continued to do so.

My wife had a younger sister, Clara, who could do no wrong in her parent's eyes and they constantly reminded Laura of how well she was doing in her life - a bigger house than us, a place in the country and a husband with a wonderful job in the city.

He was what was referred to as an engineer and apparently designed all manner of buildings for London's new skyline. Laura's sister Clara was younger by two years and they hadn't been close when they were children. This was mainly because Laura's parents had done the socially unforgivable, and had conceived her out of wedlock and had sent the child to live with an aunt in the north of the country 'out of shame' - their words. What was worse, at least for Laura, was that when the aunt died and she returned to the family home, she found she had been replaced by Clara, and was always referred to in polite company as 'cousin Laura'.

One can only imagine what effect such rejection could have on a person and Laura didn't deal with it well. Within a year of returning to what should have been the welcoming arms of her family, Laura, at the age of fifteen was 'sent abroad to a private school'.

This was at that time normally a euphemism for all manner of things, an unwanted pregnancy, an unwanted engagement, and so on, but Laura had apparently been sent to a 'private school in America' to help her with her 'education'. I also knew what *these* euphemisms meant - for private school read hospital, and for education read sanity.

Hardly surprising one might think with the way her own family treated her, but my wife was a forgiving soul and never spoke ill of her parents, not even to me. She had apparently undergone a series of treatments in 'America' but was then left there, to fend for herself and though I asked her time and again she would not tell me how she had survived such an ordeal.

I, on the other hand, wasn't so understanding with Laura's parents - I couldn't conceive how those who created someone could treat their own flesh and blood so badly, and worse, to cover the truth with lies, and all for the sake of their social standing.

I wasn't rude to them, but I was nothing more than civil. At night, after their visits I'd implore Laura to speak with them and tell them how she really felt, how she had been sent away, time and again, just for them to save face.

But Laura would not speak her mind, she smiled and was gracious with them, but now with them staying with us for goodness knew how long I felt that things needed to be resolved once and for all.

## *Chapter Five*

Thomas 1903

My marriage was settling down recently since the preceding two difficult years and Laura seemed calmer now than she had been when we'd first set up our home. I put this down to the London air suiting her and the fact that her parents didn't stay with us as much as they used to, perhaps the children growing up as well meant they didn't need their grandparents so much, and maybe they also felt that. Or perhaps they saw that it was Laura who didn't need them as much. She was approaching the age where she would receive her inheritance and I got the impression that her parents were trying not to upset her, or provoke her in any way. I didn't see why though as they had their own wealth and surely didn't need hers. Whilst they'd stopped staying for the weekends they did though still often turn up unannounced and this usually caused Laura to take to her room - the number of sudden headaches she had was staggering; and this left me to entertain them as best I could.

They were difficult people to easily socialise with and I found myself being regularly drawn into safe but long and boring conversations about the weather and politics, whilst ignoring the subjects that needed discussing between us.

Laura had pleaded with me not to challenge her parents concerning their treatment of her, saying that with time she was sure things would find their own way, and if not she would deal with them; and so, I held my counsel.

As I've said, my time at home was often limited and I was regularly called back to the hospital to assist my colleagues. This usually meant that they weren't present but had helpfully left notes with the staff telling me what needed doing in their absence.

I'd now been working at the prestigious Spellbrook Hospital in central London for about three years and enjoyed it there. The staff were friendly and wonderfully helpful, although my closer colleagues were less so if I were being totally honest. They were often stand offish and for some reason it was like they didn't trust me, though I couldn't think why - perhaps I didn't belong to the right club, but it didn't overly concern me.

The chief surgeon - a man called Sir Donald Ingram - was neither wonderful nor helpful, although he had employed both Lawrence and I on very good salaries, so I suppose I shouldn't really complain. As a junior doctor I was expected to clear patient lists of often routine procedures, and whilst I yearned for more complex tests of my skills I was prepared to bide my time until called upon.

I'd started to notice though that recently we were conducting a lot more operations than we used to, but when I asked the other surgeons, of which there were four excluding Sir Donald, why they thought that was, they never truly expressed their opinions and told me not to cause a fuss. I didn't think I was particularly, but even Lawrence said he didn't want to get into trouble with Sir Donald and that I should just let it go and carry out the work I was assigned.

As a surgeon at that time, I rarely saw patients much before an operation and not often afterwards either. I know that sounds bad, like I didn't care, but what I mean is that the nursing staff did a lot of the patient work, whilst my five colleagues and I performed the operations. I had a good staff around me as I've said, and for speed and efficiency I tried not to get too involved with pre or post op care.

To be honest as the Spellbrook catered for, how shall I say, a certain type of upper-class client, and as Sir Donald moved naturally in those circles, if a surgeon was needed pre or post op, he dealt with it. And as he signed off on everything anyway I tried not to worry about that side of things, which I thought at the time was best for all, although looking back I should have been more vigilant, and it's something I deeply regret.

There were five other surgeons at The Spellbrook Hospital - Sir Donald Ingram, the senior surgeon who had been there since time immemorial if it were to be believed. He was a man in his sixties who, according to him, had performed every operation there was to perform. He'd seen it and done it and there was nothing you could teach him or tell him. If he'd performed all that he said he had he would have to have been twice his actual age.

Then there were John Whitfield, James Radcliffe and Samuel Mortenson, all of whom had been at the hospital for some years before I was taken on, and all of whom were decent enough chaps, each extremely competent in their chosen fields, if a little over zealous in their loyalty to Sir Donald. His word was law, I was often told, and not to be countered in any way.

I'd seen them obviously in the right on numerous occasions and yet succumb to Sir Donald and his bluster. It was a strange thing to see grown men retreat in such a ready manner as these three did, but they didn't interfere in my day-to-day business and so I didn't have any real cause to tarry too much on their choices.

The last of the surgeons was my friend Lawence Jacobs. We'd grown up in the same area of London and attended medical school together many years ago - a lifetime ago it seemed, and had agreed when we graduated that we would try our hand at The Spellbrook.

Lawrence told me that his father knew the board there very well, having been a shareholder and major investor at one time. He said that as he grew up he'd often gone with his father and whilst he attended some meeting or other, had been left to amuse himself in the gardens. He said he knew the layout of the hospital as he'd often roamed about unencumbered through the wards as a younger man, often being mistaken for a junior doctor.

The Spellbrook was the most renowned surgical hospital in London and had an excellent reputation, both for its facilities and its standing in the medical profession, and so we had interviews for employment on the same day and started our careers on the same day. It was 'fate', I often said to Lawrence that our futures were intertwined in such a way and whilst he didn't disagree, he said it was more likely that they were desperate and we were the cheap option, both having so recently qualified.

Either way I'd been happy to start my career in medicine with my best friend by my side though I didn't see myself being as old as Sir Donald when I retired and had a long-term plan even on that first day which Lawrence knew about.

I felt that a surgeon's hands, whilst obviously the tools of his trade, were only good for so long and so for my long-term future I'd started teaching a small group of students whenever I operated. If I were honest I knew that eventually I'd leave surgery when my hands gave out, and instead teach others, and I thought it prudent to prepare for that progression.

I'd been honest in my initial interview and when asked had said that I'd like to go into teaching when I retired as a surgeon. Sir Donald knew of this and whilst there were rumblings at office meetings from some of the others, there was nothing wrong with a surgeon teaching the next generation and so it was permitted without too much fuss. I had the sense though that Sir Donald and his three wise men felt that their skills should be a closed shop, and that to teach the dark arts of surgery to others was allowing 'non-members' into their elite club. They often sent students out of the theatres for the most minor of reasons and I got the impression that the students weren't there to learn, but to be seen to have been there, if you understand me.

My friend Lawrence had told me more than once that a number of the board weren't happy that I taught whilst working and that that put pressure on the other surgeons, also to be so explanatory whilst operating. The students didn't ask many questions to be fair - indeed I asked them to keep their queries until after the operations were concluded and then I'd be in a better position to 'debrief' them, but the other surgeons refused to be so accommodating to the next generation and hence the subtle 'warning' from Lawrence.

## Chapter Six

The Spellbrook Hospital was under the strict supervision of Sir Donald Ingram, who was the senior surgeon and also its major shareholder. Ingram was without doubt a good surgeon, but thought himself better than he actually was, and not just in medicine, often being bombastic and overbearing with the staff for no good reason. I often assisted him but recently, more regularly I was 'taking over' from him on simple operations, 'finishing up' earlier and earlier. He seemed distracted and his manner was becoming concerning at the operating table. I'd seen him only recently make a number of mistakes on fairly straightforward procedures and it had begun to alarm me, but whenever I raised it with my other colleagues they assured me that they had seen nothing to concern them and that I should keep my comments to myself, if I knew what was good for me. This sounded to me like they were fearful of Sir Donald, but try as I might I couldn't get any of them to expand on their comments.

The Spellbrook was what was referred to as a teaching hospital and so many of the operations or procedures were viewed from the galleries above and around us as we worked and there had even been mutterings from some of the students.

Ingram talked incessantly while he operated and liked to show off his skills, but this often led to him taking risks and I felt he wasn't concentrating. I'd tried to casually offer to do more of the work whilst we were operating but he would not hear of it. I'd kept my counsel for some time but whilst we were scrubbing up one morning I took the opportunity to speak to him.

"Sir Donald, how are you this morning?"
" I am well Mr Weston, why do you ask? "
"You seem tired Sir, would you like me to take the lead on this one? "
"What? And I will assist you?"
" Yes. If that would be in order? "
"No, it would not be 'in order' Mr Weston. I do not assist, I am the senior surgeon, and I decide at my hospital who I operate on and which operations I carry out. Do I make myself clear? "
"Yes Sir Donald, it's just that…"
" It's just what? Spit it out man, I haven't got all day"

"Very well. You have been making mistakes...you've seemed...distracted, that's all. Is everything alright Sir? That's all I'm asking"

"Mr Weston. Listen to me, for I will say this only once. I'm fully functional thank you. I do not make mistakes, and if you wish to continue here you will keep your comments to yourself. I know that you have been going round agitating my staff and I will not let it continue."

" Agitating Sir Donald? I have not been agitating, I am concerned for you that's all. We all overwork ourselves sometimes Sir Donald, we can all become tired, a little slower perhaps to react to situations, there is no shame..."

"Well, that is very kind of you I am sure to be concerned for me but now I will ask you to step down Mr Weston"

"I'm sorry?"

" Step down. Mr Jacobs! " Sir Donald called over his shoulder.

Another surgeon, my friend Lawrence Jacobs appeared behind us.

"Sir Donald?"

" Scrub up Mr Jacobs, you will assist me today "

"Sir Donald? I thought Mr Weston..?"

" Do you want to learn something Mr Jacobs or not? Scrub up man. I haven't got time for a debate. Mr Weston has decided he does not wish to learn from me and has requested to be replaced"
"Yes Sir Donald." Lawrence did as he was told and I moved aside to let him get to one of the sinks. As he passed he looked questioningly at me. All I could do was mouth 'be careful' at him.

I was in my office some hours later when the door burst open.

"Thomas! Help, now, quickly!" Lawrence stood there still in his theatre gown; blood smeared all over the front of it. It wasn't unusual to see a surgeon with *some* blood on his hands and down his front, but never this much.

" What on earth…? " I began.
"Come quickly Thomas, for God's sake, before it's too late!"

I rose from my desk and followed my friend down to the theatres. Lawrence wasn't a man to panic and I hadn't seen him so pale in all the years I'd known him.

"Lawrence? What is it? What's happened?"
"It's Sir Donald…"
"What? What's happened Lawrence? Is he alright?" There was a panic in his eyes and as we ran into the theatre I could see why.

Sir Donald stood in his usual position but there was blood all over the floor, flowing over the edge of the operating table. This was a simple operation - a spleen removal, and there was no need for all this blood, not unless something had gone badly wrong.

Sir Donald casually looked up and with his hands still within the cavity of the patient on the table he nodded at me, beckoning me towards him. The look on his face wasn't of a man who was in control, but rather one that seemed not to care.

"Ah Mr Weston, good of you to come. Finish up here would you? There's a good man, Mr Jacobs seems to have made a bit of a mess with this poor chap, and he's making a lot of fuss over a little bit of blood". He said as more of the patient's had the audacity to drip on the surgeon's immaculate shoes.
"Sir Donald…I haven't…you said…"

"Now now, Mr Jacobs, there will be time for a debrief later I'm sure. Mr Weston, don't be shy, scrub up please and jump in as soon as you like, I need to change my shoes now before I dine tonight"

Ingram looked at me and nodded to Lawrence

"Thank you Mr Jacobs, rinse off and wait for me in my office please, I will be with you shortly"
"But Sir Donald…?"
"Thank you Mr Jacobs that will be all, you've done quite enough for one day."

Lawrence paused briefly, he wasn't the sort of man who would argue in public and certainly wouldn't cross Sir Donald in an operating theatre, but I could tell he wasn't happy with whatever had gone on.
      Having 'scrubbed up' I approached the operating table and saw that the patient was almost fully awake, though the operation was nowhere near completed.

"Nurse! Put this man under for God's sake he must be in agony"
"Sir Donald?" The nurse looked questioningly at him

"Nurse. Do as I say, now. How this man is not screaming in pain I don't know…put him under again" I nearly shouted at her. I got the impression that the poor man on the operating table had never been given anaesthetic, as there were certainly no signs of it having been administered.

Again, the nurse looked at Ingram, who hadn't moved from the table. With a sigh and a slight nod, he agreed with me and the nurse did what I'd asked.

"Where are the students Sir Donald?" I asked as I stemmed the flow of blood and looked at what needed to be done.
"I sent them out" he said matter of factly
"Sent them out? Why? Surely this is a straightforward though interesting procedure for them to watch Sir Donald?"
"I sent them out, Mr Weston, as I did not wish to have them here. A simple straightforward matter, as you say, and I'm sure the students have seen this type of procedure many times before. It was unnecessary to have them here, even if it was me performing it"
"But they were here earlier Sir Donald?"
"Yes, and I sent them out. Shall we get on Mr Weston?"

## *Chapter Seven*

"Sir Donald. I'm quite happy to finish up here" I'd said many times during the last hour of the procedure, but he wouldn't have it.

"Mr Weston. We will conclude here and then I will see both you and Mr Jacobs in my office - perhaps a little debrief and a catch up - we haven't seen each other for a while have we?"

"No Sir, we haven't - we've both been busy" though I actually wanted to say that it was I who had been the busy one. I hadn't seen Ingram for weeks before today. He apparently had had overseas business to attend to, but no one I asked could categorically state what it entailed or where that business was, although the city of Boston had been mentioned.

We finished the 'simple' operation, or rather I did, with Ingram hovering over me, hurrying me along. It was almost as if he wanted to be somewhere else, as if he had urgent business there and that this poor man on the operating table was an inconvenience to him. As soon as the last stitch was in place Ingram dropped his redundant scalpel on the man's chest and walked out.

I had no notes about who the patient was and asked the staff to attend to the after care, which was standard. I asked the senior nurse to ensure that his family were made aware of the success of the operation but this was met with a look of confusion and then a small nod.

I washed up and looked around for Lawrence in his office, but he wasn't there. Perhaps he was already having his own debrief with Ingram, being lectured on the errors 'he' had made, but I knew that those errors were more likely to be Ingram's rather than Lawence's. Lawrence was a diligent and conscientious surgeon, he rarely rushed a procedure, no matter how small and I saw the way he looked at Ingram having been 'stood down'.

I made my way to Ingram's office and waited outside, like an errant schoolboy. As I sat in the corridor it reminded me of my first day at the Spellbrook, sitting in avid anticipation and then having been treated to the full tour by the top man himself - Sir Donald. What a difference a few short years made, I thought. When I'd first met him he was a fulsome host, full of pride in 'his' hospital, 'his' staff and I must admit I was taken in by it - it was my first proper employment and I was impressed by the whole thing.

But having worked the hours I had over the past few years and having seen the short cuts Ingram took when he was actually at the hospital I was no longer impressed by him.

I decided then and there that this was no longer the environment I wanted to work in and I felt it was time to move on. That thought gave me a confidence that I wouldn't perhaps naturally have had and it would make me braver in my dealings with Ingram and his 'three wise men' as I called them, if only to myself, from now on.

As I sat there I heard raised voices from within Ingram's office

"...Sir Donald, how can you say that? How can you blame me? I didn't have any prep notes, you called me in at the last minute and then I had to recover what *you* had done, not I. I did not sever the artery Sir - you did!"
"I most certainly did not Mr Jacobs, and I will remind you to whom you are speaking. This is my hospital and I say what goes. If you needed preparatory notes on such a simple operation you perhaps are not the surgeon I thought you were when I employed you"

"A simple operation? It would have been simple had you started it correctly - it's almost like you were somewhere else - your mind certainly was not in that theatre Sir. I told you time and again the man was in no fit state to have his spleen removed, and why in any event? Why him? Why then specifically? He wasn't even on the patient list for the day?"

"Mr Jacobs. There are certain patients as you know, who do not appear on any lists, they do not *need* to appear on any lists. You have been aware of this for some time, and you have benefitted from our arrangements, have you not?"

"Yes. I have been aware of it, but I do not agree with it. I know you have assisted me in my…troubles Sir Donald, and I am grateful, but that man nearly died. If Thomas had not come when he did…that man…"

"That man? That man was not important Mr Jacobs, only his spleen was, and it was saved. I will leave you to make the necessary arrangements for its transfer and if, you have calmed down sufficiently you may assist me tomorrow when we transplant it"

"What if he had died, Sir Donald, another one? What then..?"

"I will bid you goodnight Mr Jacobs. I have matters to attend to at my club and I do not need you delaying me any further. Do not concern yourself with things that are way beyond you".

The door suddenly opened and closed and then Lawrence stood before me, his eyes pointed up to the heavens and his breathing heavy.

"Lawrence? What was all that about? Are you alright?"
"Oh, Thomas I'm sorry, I didn't see you there. Are you waiting to speak to the 'great man' - 'our wonderful benefactor?' I shouldn't waste your time waiting any further my friend, he's already left for his club"
"No, he's still in his office surely? You were just talking to him?"
"No. He used the back stairs. He always does when he wants to avoid things, or people who would cause him problems"
"But Lawrence, what was that conversation all about? What's this about transplants? What was he saying?"

"Don't get involved Thomas, that would be my advice. While he has no hold on you perhaps a decent reference would be a better thing to ask him about?"

"What do you mean Lawrence?"

"I'm saying that it might be better to get away from all of this whilst you can, it's a bad business. You need to move on and not get involved. It's too late for me, and the others - Radcliffe, Whitfield and Mortenson, we're trapped - he tapped into what we needed and now has us in his grasp, but you? You can still leave; you don't owe him anything"

"But where would I go? Laura and I are trying for more children. I can't just leave, but what do you mean, 'tapped in to?' What hold does he have over you? I can't imagine?"

Lawrence stood with his head down, his friend before him. Should he tell him the truth, and try and get out himself, or was he way beyond that? He was aware that Ingram knew a lot of wealthy and important people who he'd helped for many years - with their own health and that of their families.

Ingram was a dinosaur when it came to the running of the hospital, but in many other ways so ahead of his time and he'd profited greatly from his medical prowess.

Years ago, he'd pioneered a number of ground-breaking operations, some of which just saved limbs, but others which truly changed and saved lives, and he was always pushing, searching for the next success, the next medical miracle.

But the problem with Ingram was that whilst he sometimes had wonderful miraculous successes, there were an awful lot of failures and he'd been running out of willing patients, but then a medical miracle had dropped into his lap, or rather a financial opportunity as he saw it.

An 'institution' on the other side of the city needed to close - the owners had been running it almost as a charity for years and their willingness to put their hands in their pockets any more was coming to an end. Ingram saw this as a chance to continue his work whilst outwardly enhancing his philanthropic reputation, and that of The Spellbrook as being the number one hospital in the city.

And so, he 'generously' negotiated taking almost two hundred of the most needy and disturbed long-term patients and housing them at his hospital. Outwardly the new residents would be treated with the best care and attention money could provide, with qualified and specially trained staff all day and all night.

But in reality, the patients were used, almost immediately by Ingram and the other surgeons, including Lawrence, as guinea pigs for rehearsing new operations.

The only surgeon not involved and not made aware of what was happening was Thomas, and that was why his daily lists were heavier - for as he cleared the backlogs of standard procedures Ingram and his colleagues worked mainly downstairs - practising and perfecting transplants for profit.

Lawrence paused but then said "Gambling, Thomas. He has covered a large number of my gambling debts, and so it's not as easy for me to just walk away. Believe me I would if I could, but I can't - but you? You can, and I'd urge you to do that, before it's too late."

*Chapter Eight*

Lawrence had left me there, outside Ingrams office, shutting the door behind him and as he walked away from me I knew things weren't right with him, let alone at the hospital. I'd known Lawrence for too long to just accept what he'd said as the real reason for his strange behaviour. And as I sat in the corridor I felt Lawrence was holding back, not telling me the things he truly felt, and not telling me the truth in any event, which wasn't like him at all - I thought he trusted me more than that. There had been no threats from Ingram that I'd heard, but surely the hold he had over Lawrence was more than just gambling debts, Lawrence had always had debts and they hadn't bothered him before. And in any event why would Ingram pay them off for him? No, there had to be something else, but try as I might I couldn't think what it might be, only one thing made sense and I did not want to think that of my friend.

Ingram and Lawrence had talked of transplants? But why was that? It was still science fiction surely? But they talked about it like it was commonplace.

I certainly hadn't performed any transplants, and although the theory itself was straightforward, and easy to understand when written or drawn in a book or medical paper, the actual practice was surely impossible?

Although man had dreamt of being able to replace worn out limbs and organs prolonging the life of a man by perhaps decades, modern medicine was years away from perfecting such things.

But if I wasn't performing them, then were Ingram and the others doing them, while I was conducting all the routine operations? Surely it wasn't possible? When had they learnt such skills? And where were these operations being carried out, I had not seen any sign of them when I was at The Spellbrook, so there must be somewhere else - another hospital where they could work secretly?

Were Lawrence and the others performing transplants for money, or was it just Ingram performing them and paying others to keep quiet? I couldn't believe that Lawrence would be involved in something like this. Was this the hold Ingram had over Lawrence though, and the others? And if off the book operations were taking place here, who were the transplants for, and, more importantly I felt, who were the donors?

It couldn't go on, but what was I to do? If I raised the issue to the board without proof I'd be ridiculed and probably hounded out of the hospital, and definitely sued by Ingram. Surgery was all I knew, and so I was determined to find the proof even if finding it would probably lead to me leaving the Spellbrook anyway.

If I were honest I'd say that I'd been somewhat unsettled at the hospital for a while, and had been studying a new field called 'psychology', in what little spare time I had, and it was something that had started to interest me. Perhaps I'd need it as a back up to surgery if that was taken away from me.

I'd started to read papers written by a new type of doctor, with a new way of thinking and whilst it was relatively new in itself - only being founded in modern times as late at the eighteen fifties, the concept had been around since Greek times and perhaps I thought as a discipline I should open myself up to its possibilities.

I surprised even myself in this thinking as I'd always been a body first type of doctor as I've said, perhaps I'd need to change my *own* way of thinking. In the meantime, though I'd consider what I was to do and discuss it with Laura as for me to walk away from the Spellbrook would cause severe financial problems for us both.

## *Chapter Nine*

It was blissfully quiet in the house today, a few days after I'd overheard Ingram and Lawrence arguing. The children had gone to the park with their grandparents and as Lawrence had been working again all night at the hospital he was staying at our house and sleeping in late. I knew Laura was somewhere upstairs but I didn't know exactly where.

I sat in the front parlour, as the sun always caught this room in the mornings, and I liked to sit with a newspaper and see what was happening in the world, but I didn't read much of today's news though - if truth be told I was looking for a way out of my current position at The Spellbrook and perhaps a change of direction, career wise and I couldn't concentrate on the print before me.

I'd been at the hospital for about three years now and whilst the work kept me busy I felt I wasn't progressing as I thought I should be, but now I was starting to understand why. We'd always had regular office meetings - during which Sir Donald, the other surgeons and senior members of the nursing staff discussed the weekly status of the hospital and any particular problems, but nothing ever really changed, no one wanted to progress the hospital the way I felt it should progress, but now I knew that this was because they were obviously too busy making money to add outward development of the hospital to their agenda. There were modern methods and procedures being discovered all the time in medicine but Ingram wouldn't hear of openly introducing them at 'his hospital', as it would take too much training and cost too much, he'd always said.

Therefore, things stagnated for everyone else, and it was almost as if time itself was standing still. But while he was stopping progress for everyone else, he was in reality, expanding the boundaries of medicine every day, for himself and his 'friends' and becoming wealthier every day in the process, albeit totally illegally.

I hadn't yet discussed my thoughts with Laura, and I *couldn't* discuss the matter of illegal transplants with my wife - it would shock her too much, and so, for her own sanity I remained silent, preferring to allude to the fact that I felt a change was needed for my *own*. I thought overall she'd want me to be happy in what I did and would probably agree with my decision if it were to leave The Spellbrook.

I also hadn't mentioned anything more to Lawrence since the other day, but he'd previously known that I wasn't happy, and now, since his admissions about transplants, he surely couldn't expect me to do nothing. He'd said wait, until he'd spoken to Ingram, but what was he going to say to him? He'd hardly be happy that I knew what was going on. He wasn't a reasonable man, and wouldn't listen to Lawrence, no matter what he said to him.

During previous office meetings I'd been the only dissenting voice against Sir Donald when he preached his mantras of 'carry on as we are' and 'that's the way we've always done it'. That had only been in relation to procedural changes that seemed progressive to me and good for the hospital, and no one else ever spoke up regarding even those - imagine if I were to raise this concern, this outrage, especially to a full board of shareholders, no, I thought it best to have some actual proof before I spoke.

If I was being honest, I'd been disappointed with Lawrence in the past that he hadn't spoken up before now, not once to back me up, preferring instead to look down at his feet or anywhere else other than my eye.

I had chided him when we were alone and he'd reminded me that Ingram had a hold over him and the other surgeons. But now I knew that things were a little more complicated than just me being the only one pushing for change, and I also knew I wouldn't be able to rely on Lawrence - I was on my own.

    I'd always known that I'd never have the support of the 'three wise men' against Ingram, but now it would seem, my lifelong friend would always side with them and Ingram, and so I found myself in a no-win situation - perhaps my only choice *would* be to leave The Spellbrook.

    I knew though that if I tried to leave The Spellbrook quietly and on my own terms Ingram would stop me working at another hospital. 'His hospital' was the pinnacle of medicine in his view, and to go anywhere else was an obvious step down, and he wouldn't want questions being asked as to why one of his surgeons had voluntarily left his employ. I'm sure that he'd also make it known to any potential employer that I'd failed in some way and that would prevent me from working elsewhere. I'd seen him do this to doctors in the past and knew he'd do it to me without hesitation, and whilst it wasn't the type of hold he had over Lawrence or the others, it was a hold nevertheless.

I got up, thinking now was as good a time as any to speak to Laura and make her aware of my decision. I could hear her voice somewhere upstairs but who was she speaking to I wondered?

Walking up the stairs I heard hushed voices and what I thought was 'if you tell him I'll kill you!' from my wife.

As I reached the landing I saw Laura closing Lawrence's bedroom door and if ever there was a personification of a guilty look then this was it.

"Hello my love, is everything alright?" I asked her
" Oh yes Thomas, everything's fine" she replied "I was just taking Lawrence some tea as he'd woken up"
"That's kind, but is everything well - I thought I heard harsh words?"
" Oh. You weren't supposed to hear that. Lawrence was joking with me about telling you what the children and I were going to buy you for your birthday"
"Oh? And you'd kill him for telling me?"
" No. Of course not Thomas, it was just an expression, I wouldn't hurt Lawrence. I'm going to see the children now; I'll see you soon" she said as she pecked me on the cheek and went down the stairs.

I knocked on Lawrence's door and entered to find him sitting up in bed and drinking the tea Laura had brought him.

"Morning my friend, how was the night shift?"
" Busy at best, appalling at worst Thomas. Ingram is a slavedriver he really is. He expects his theatres to be bloody production lines, not places of treatment and caring"
"Then why don't you do something about it Lawrence? Tell him you've had enough. You won't be part of his illegal money-making enterprise anymore"
"You know why Thomas; you know exactly why. I'm an addict and I can't just stop. He pays my debts Thomas I've told you that"
"But that doesn't make sense - your debts can't be that bad? Surely you can walk away? I'm looking at getting out…I'll lend you the money, how much do you need?"
" Getting out? Getting out of what? The Spellbrook? "
"Yes. I'm looking at quitting, going abroad, starting again. There are great opportunities overseas, America, Lawrence, come with me, come and be free, far away from Ingram and 'his hospital '. What do you say?"

" Have you discussed this with Laura? "

"No…not yet"

"And Ingram?"

" No…not yet. But I will, in time. I need to speak to Laura, and see what's out there. It might have to be in a new field though"

"A new field? What do you mean?"

"Not surgery. I think Ingram will put a block on that, even overseas, don't you? "

"Probably. Look, Thomas, don't do anything rash, don't say anything just yet. Let me see if I can't talk to Ingram, sound him out, what do you say?"

" I'd say you're mad, my friend. Can you imagine him letting you or me just walk away? "

"No. But he might give you a decent reference, it's worth a try"

"I wouldn't have thought so, but let me write to a few places first, good hospitals abroad, see what might be available, for two surgeons…"

" I don't know Thomas, one, he might let go but two? Definitely not!"

## *Chapter Ten*

Following what I'd overheard Lawrence and Ingram arguing about I'd decided to make my own enquiries, though I didn't outright believe it, as surely it couldn't be true. The whole nursing staff wouldn't allow it; but was there perhaps a small group of that staff who knew what was happening at The Spellbrook and said nothing for fear of repercussions? But what repercussions would be so bad that they wouldn't say anything? There was no way that Ingram could have a hold over all of them? There were far too many people working here to cover up such a thing.

As I've said as a surgeon I didn't ordinarily visit patients, at least not until I'd operated on them and then in all honesty to ensure that they were still alive - no I'm joking! What I mean is that I didn't go to them in the normal course of events, they came to me, usually already sedated and prepared for whatever surgery was necessary.

However, when I started to hear these rumours of transplants happening at the hospital I'd been so proud to represent, confirmed by Lawrence, I started to visit the wards on my days off. I saw no signs of transplants amongst the patients upstairs and so made my way to the Psychiatric Ward which unfortunately was in the basement of the hospital. I say unfortunately as the damp that pervaded from the walls and floors and the poor lighting only added to the grim feel of the place and would have done nothing to aid the recovery or at the very least, the mental stability of the poor souls housed there. As I understood things, the board had effectively won a contract from the Government to house two hundred 'long term' patients at the Spellbrook when a purpose-built hospital, on the other side of the city, had closed suddenly. The Spellbrook wasn't built for such patients and there were few doctors or staff adequately trained to help them and so the ward had the air of a Victorian asylum where people were kept subdued and incarcerated for long periods of time. I was ashamed to say that I rescued no one from that particular hell hole that night, and what I did may have made things that much worse for them.

Having visited the Psychiatric Ward I found that there were fewer patients than I expected there and many of them seemed to have been operated on - were these the transplant patients?

Most were heavily sedated and the nurses, who seemed to be a mixture of former women's prison jailers and natural born sadists, shepherded me out of their empire, it seemed almost as soon as I'd arrived in it and had started asking questions.

I felt it my duty to immediately bring these matters to the attention of the board at our next meeting - even if Sir Donald was involved, the shareholders needed to know, as did the outside world.

It was therefore to my surprise when, the following day an emergency staff meeting was called, by whom I didn't know but I suspected it was Ingram, no doubt alerted to my previous night's visit to the underground hell of the Psychiatric Ward.

Ingram called the meeting to order

"Gentlemen, I have called this emergency staff meeting as there is one amongst us who seems intent on ruining the good name of The Spellbrook…"
"Sir Donald…" I interjected
"Mr Weston, you will wait until I have finished before you speak, do I make myself clear?"
"Yes Sir Donald" I seethed

"One who believes it is necessary to involve himself in matters which do not concern him..."
"Now wait a minute Sir Donald..."
"Mr Weston, one more interruption and I will ask you to leave - you will have your turn"
"Very well"
"I have called this meeting to put things to a vote. I assure all those present that the outcome of the vote will be kept within this room and that no man's decision will go against him, if that is his true feeling. Do you all understand what I am saying?"

There were, unsurprisingly, four nods around the table. I put my hand in the air.

"Mr Weston. What do you not understand about what I have said?"
"May I speak freely Sir Donald?"
"No, you may not. I had not finished. The question was, do you understand that your vote will be just as important as the next man's?"
"I understand that Sir Donald, but I severely doubt it"
"Then I will finish. These are the facts gentlemen. Last night a member of the senior staff went to a ward that they had no reason to go to. This was to the considerable disturbance and distress of the

patients who reside there, and to the great detriment of the staff they encountered who do a fine job, an excellent job in difficult circumstances. This staff member alerted no other staff member to their intentions and consequently breached a basic tenet of their contract with the hospital and medicine generally. As chair and part owner of the hospital it is my responsibility to ensure that all staff and patients at this wonderful establishment are looked after as if they were family, and that their safety and well-being is always at the forefront of our minds. To my utter dismay and sadness, I have to report that a member of this staff breached that trust and must be dealt with accordingly. Mr Weston, I am obviously meaning you, but before you speak I will put things to a vote - a vote of your peers - I will take no part in the vote as I would hate to be accused of influencing your colleagues in any way. Gentlemen, may I ask, with a show of hands who believes that stern action must be taken in these heinous circumstances."

Immediately four hands went up in the air - even Lawrence, who with a mouthed apology looked downwards.

"Then it is decided Mr Weston. You will be immediately suspended from working at The Spellbrook until further notice. I will consult our solicitors and see on what terms we can dispense with your services, unless you would like to be a gentleman about this all and resign?"

I have to say I was tempted to resign on the spot as I knew I was fighting a losing battle, if not a lost one, but instead, and to my shame I used words that I will not repeat in print, and knocking my chair over backwards as I rose, I called Ingram words that you would not normally hear in polite circles, and most of them not medically correct or probably physically possible.

## Chapter Eleven

Following my suspension from the hospital I made a number of decisions. One of those decisions was that I would be honest with my wife and tell her what I suspected. I found Laura in the drawing room and sat down next to her.

"Thomas, good morning. I thought you were at the hospital?"
"No. I'm not. I fear I won't be going there again"
"Why? What's happened?"
"I've been suspended, pending an enquiry"
"An enquiry? An enquiry into what?"
"Into my actions. Which I believed were justified. And when I tell you what I found, what has been happening, I think you'll believe I was justified as well"
"Thomas. You're scaring me. What on earth has happened?"
"Laura, I need you to be strong as I need to speak plainly to you",

"Very well, my love. I think I'm stronger than you think, but please tell me what's troubling you"
"I've been speaking to Lawrence"
"...Yes"
"About what happened at the Spellbrook"
"Oh? Thomas! Please, don't believe what that man says. It will all be lies"
"Laura! He's my friend. Please calm yourself, let me speak"
"No, my love, I can't. He's not the man you think he is. I can explain, I will tell you the truth. I haven't always, and for good reason, but please, hear me out"
"So, you know…?"
"Yes, of course I know. I was there when it happened?"
"Even then? My God! Well, it hasn't stopped Laura, since you were there. It's still happening"
"He is an evil man, Thomas. I knew he was. I never want him in our house again! Those poor people!"
"What? No, I think he was acting under orders, I don't think he had any choice, and Ingram has a hold over him now"
"Orders? What are you saying?" Laura asked
"It's the only reason such things would be allowed to happen" I assured her

"There were others there as well. When it happened. Every time. Thomas please do not think badly of me. There was nothing I could do. I was restrained, when I was unruly"

"I know my love, but there was nothing you could do. You couldn't have known they were performing transplants - who could?"

"Transplants? Thomas, what are you talking about? Transplants of what?"

"That I don't know, but the other night I went downstairs, at the Spellbrook…"

"Oh Thomas…why? Why did you do that? The conditions were awful - why would you put yourself through that?"

"I had to know. I had to see the truth"

"About…transplants?"

"Yes. Involuntary transplants - there were people there, long term patients, with operation scars, wounds in need of dressing and most of those poor people just lying there, suffering beyond belief, and no staff attending to them!"

"Stop it Thomas, please stop it!"

"I know you suffered, in your younger days, in that awful place…but what were you meaning? What did you see?"

"…Thomas…I…I witnessed…things. Horrific things, which had an effect on me, made me question my own sanity. You cannot imagine"

"I'm sure I couldn't my love. But your suffering is over. You are safe now, and among those who love you. Let us talk about it no more"

"I agree. But don't listen to that man, promise me Thomas?"

"I can't promise that Laura, not if he sees the error of his ways and helps me when I go to the police, as I must."

I *had* decided to go to the police about my findings about the Spellbrook and the illegal practices that had been happening there. I felt if I acted quickly then the police would find the evidence that would have Ingram and the others sent to prison for a long time, albeit I knew that that would include Lawrence as well. But he must have known the risks, he was an intelligent man after all and must have considered the dangers of what he was doing. But operating on mentally ill patients? Surely he hadn't thought that through and considered it at all reasonable? He must accept the consequences as Ingram and the others must - whatever they may be.

I made my way to the police station and spoke to the desk sergeant there. Having asked to speak to an Inspector I sat and waited for some considerable time. Eventually a plain clothes officer opened the door and beckoned me inside, to an interview room, where we sat at a battered desk.

"Mr Weston?"

"Doctor Weston, yes, Thomas Weston"

"I am Detective Sergeant Aldergather and I've been told that you have some concerns about a hospital, Sir?"

"Concerns? Well, yes, I suppose you could say they are concerns. Have you been told everything Sergeant?"

"Mr Weston…Doctor Weston. I have been told that you were recently suspended by the board of the Spellbrook hospital for making a number of unauthorised visits to a ward?"

"But that's not a police matter Sergeant…?"

"Ah good, that's agreed then" the Sergeant said as he stood up and extended his hand to me

"No. I mean, the visits weren't in accordance with the hospital guidelines admittedly…but"

"So, they *were* unauthorised then?"

"Well…yes"

"So, they were unauthorised. And I understand you saw hospital patients with operation scars Sir?"

"Well…yes"

"In a hospital?"

"Yes…but"

"This is truly shocking, Sir. A hospital full of patients, who have been operated on. Truly shocking, the crime of the century surely? Now, if there's nothing else Sir?"

"I don't like your tone Sergeant"

"And I don't like my time being wasted, Sir"

"I'd like to speak to someone else"

"So would I, Mr Weston. Now, if you'll excuse me, I do have proper crimes to solve. I understand you're no longer in the employ of the hospital in any event?"

"I am currently suspended, that's true"

"Look, Doctor Weston, if you have any proof, come back and see us, ask for me, if you want, but until then, I'd let things lie if I were you. I'll let the Inspector know and I'm sure he'll mention it at his club?"

"His club?"

"His club, Sir. If you get my meaning?"

"I don't"

"You will, Sir, in time, of that I'm sure"

And with that I was offered the police officer's hand again and then the exit door.

So, the police wouldn't help me, and potentially all I had done was alert Ingram that I was serious in my intention to stop him and his associates from making money out of other people's misery. I would write to the hospital board and let them deal with it.

    I knew though in doing so I would be finished as a surgeon - no one would employ me after that, not with Ingram's influence in the profession, but that was something I would have to come to terms with and deal with if and when it happened.

## Chapter Twelve

I was in a deep and wonderful sleep some nights later when I was rudely awoken by my father-in-law at my bedside.

I'd been walking on a sunlit beach with Laura, two children playing in the sea by our side. The sun was setting but I couldn't work out where we were. I knew it wasn't England - for although the sun was low, it was still too warm on our faces and the sand beneath our feet too white, too pure to be a local beach…

"Thomas! Thomas! Wake up! You're needed at the hospital, there's been a railway accident and they're calling everyone in. Quickly, get dressed, there's a carriage waiting for you downstairs"
"What? Where am I…?"
"Wake up, quickly now, I've told them to wait for you, get dressed"

Laura murmured in her sleep and rolled over, pulling a pillow over her head, shushing me and her father, even though we were only whispering.

"What time is it?" I asked my father-in-law
"Just gone two o'clock - quickly Thomas. I'm going back to bed. We have a long journey tomorrow…I mean, today"

I was still drowsy and as I dressed I couldn't help but wonder which train had crashed at such an hour, but if the hospital called for me then I must go, there was no doubt about that, it was my duty as a doctor.

I lifted the pillow that covered her and kissed Laura on the back of the head, told her that I would see her soon and to kiss the children for me - a ritual I had whenever I left for work.

I went downstairs and quietly opened and closed the front door. It was the last time I was to step foot inside that house for the events of that night set me on a path that was to lead me to where I am now.

I got in the carriage and apologised to the driver for keeping him waiting.

"No worries Doctor - the hospital then is it?"
"Yes apparently so, as quick as you can please"" I began as the carriage lurched off down the street.

Although I normally walked to work I knew that the hospital was only a ten-minute drive in a carriage and although I dozed, it felt like we'd been travelling for much longer than that.

"Driver! Driver! Where are you going? This isn't the way to the hospital"
"It is Sir - the Hampton Hospital"
"The Hampton? Why on earth are we going to the Hampton? I work at the Spellbrook. I need to go to the Spellbrook"
"Oh no Sir - I'm told they're taking all the people to the Hampton - they've asked for all surgeons to go there"
"Who are *they*? Who's running this show?"
"I wouldn't know Sir - I'm just a driver - I just do what I 'm told"

The carriage was travelling at quite a pace and as the driver wouldn't stop there wasn't much I could do about the situation, but sit back and wait for him to reach our destination and stop.
    We eventually pulled up at the hospital, but it didn't look like one that was coping with a recent influx of train accident casualties, unless I was arriving after they'd already been taken inside.

I alighted from the carriage, ignoring the driver's outstretched hand as he touched his cap to me. I wasn't going to tip him for bringing me here and I presumed he'd already been paid to collect me.

As I walked up the driveway I got the distinct impression that something was wrong. It should have been busier, so much busier than what I was currently seeing. There were no ambulances lined up outside, no harried porters or nurses running about, shepherding people in, or consoling bereaved relatives on benches as I'd thought there would be.

As I entered the foyer I saw something I hadn't expected at all either. There was peace and tranquillity, which was unheard of in a hospital. There were no screams from traumatised patients, or loud singing from drunks slumped on the floor - there was nothing.

I approached a nurse who sat on the reception desk and who laid down her newspaper looking at me with surprise.

"Can I help you Sir?" she asked, genuinely taken aback by someone approaching her. I think it was more the hour of the intrusion rather than anything else, but it was almost as if I had invaded her leisure time.

"Good morning nurse. I'm Thomas Weston"
"Good for you Sir. Can I help you?" she repeated
"I was told to come here"
"And you have succeeded. What can I do for you Sir?"
"I have come to assist with the accident? I'm a surgeon."
"The accident Sir? This isn't that sort of hospital, this is a teaching hospital"
"The train crash?"
"Oh my God, has there been a train crash? Where? How bad is it? You probably need to get to the Spellbrook, or one of those types of hospitals - they're more likely to deal with that I would have thought?"
"But I was told to come here…well I wasn't…I was told…" I trailed off.

I turned away from the desk, lost in thought. Why had I been told to come here, but then remembered I hadn't been. I hadn't actually been told to come anywhere. I'd been told a carriage was waiting for me, and it was, and the driver brought me here - but why, for what purpose?

"Ah Mr Weston" a booming voice came from the back of the foyer. "Would you follow me please?"
"I'm sorry, who are you?" I asked the man as he walked away from me.
He was dressed from head to toe in black and looked attired for the worst winter known to man. I couldn't see his face, but then I recognised the voice - Sir Donald.

"Don't be long - some of us need our sleep Mr Weston"
"Sir Donald? I don't understand? What are you doing here? Are you helping with the train crash as well?"
"Weston, you really are quite dense aren't you? There is no train crash. No need for your great expertise. No. I wanted to bring you here to show you something"
"Really?" I said hesitantly. I didn't trust Ingram and hadn't for a while, but he was effectively paying my wages for the time being and so I went with him.

We walked through to a refectory area where having preceded me he sat at a table. He kept his gloves on and I got the impression he wasn't staying very long. Having looked at the grimy table between us, he placed his hat on his knee.

"Weston. Have I not helped you?"

"Yes Sir Donald, you have in the past"

"Have I not been kind to you?"

"Well…kind..? Sir Donald, what's this about? It's three o'clock in the morning, why are we here?"

"I am well aware what time it is Weston. The same as I am well aware that you have been telling tales"

"Tales? What on earth..?"

"Tales Weston. Tales. Like some upset schoolgirl. You either do not realise, or do not care what damage you may do to the Spellbrook. Personally, for your sake, I hope it's that you do not realise what you have done. Were it that you do not care…well that would be a whole different matter. I have brought you here to show you what sort of place you could work at if it were not for me"

"I'm sorry Sir Donald. I have no idea what you're talking about"

"How many times have I told you to keep your opinions to yourself Weston?"

"Many times. And that's very clear, you don't want to hear anyone else's opinion. It's only your opinion that matters doesn't it?"

"I will not deign to give that statement any response Weston. You are, and have always been above your station. Do you realise how long it has taken me to build the Spellbrook up to where it is now? How much of my own money I have spent to bring it to what it is now? Do you have any idea? Or is it that you do not care? Compared to my position at the hospital, what do you matter? What does your opinion matter?"

"If that's an actual question? It's my opinion Sir Donald that a surgeon, like any other doctor, first does no harm, wouldn't you agree?"

"Obviously"

"To anyone, regardless of who they are?"

"Get on with it - what do you mean?"

"I know what you and the others have been doing"

"Doing? What on earth do you mean, doing? Stop talking in riddles man"

"Operating on mentally ill people, who don't need an operation, and removing their organs for profit. That's what I mean. Are they the tales you think I was telling? How could you do such things? You are supposed to be a man of medicine"

"Weston. Weston, please calm down. Please show some decorum. Let me ask you - who has listened to you?"

"Obviously no one"

"Obviously. And do you know why?"

"Because of who you are"

"Because of who I am, and the fact that you are talking nonsense - where is your proof? No-one would ever believe you, even if it were true. Transplants indeed?"

"None of the others have the stomach to go up against you, but by saying nothing, and going along with you, they're just as bad as you. I know you've been conducting horrendous procedures on the people downstairs, without anaesthetic, and with little or no preparation…"

"Oh, your students? Did they tell you this"?

"No. I've seen it for myself. As you know I went to the Psychiatric Ward the other night"

"I know that you did Weston. But what did you actually see? Where is your proof?"

"I have none at the moment, but I will get it. I will let the authorities know what has been going on"

"The authorities? Like the police? Haven't you already tried that? I haven't heard them rushing to kick in the doors of my hospital, have you?"

"News travels quickly, doesn't it? But tell me - what hold do you have over the others - Lawrence Jacobs, and the others - your three wise men?"

"Hold? I have no hold over them Weston. They can walk away any time they wish. I would not stop them"

"No, they cannot - they are each beholden to you in some way - Jacobs - how much of Lawrence's gambling debts have you paid off for him?"
"Gambling debts?"
"Yes. He told me - you have been paying off his gambling debts"
"Is that what he's told you Weston? Let me assure you I would not give that man a penny of my hard-earned money, not one penny. Ask him about what it is that actually motivates him…and it has nothing to do with money"
"Motivates him? What do you mean?"
"Ah, here he is now - why don't you ask him yourself?"

The door opened and my friend, my closest friend for so many years, walked in. He walked slowly and held his hat between his hands, his head hung low.

"Ah, Thomas, you are here, please…listen, I can explain…"
"Lawrence - tell me this isn't true? Tell me he forced you, threatened you?"

"No Thomas. He didn't. To my ultimate shame, there was no force on Sir Donald's part, he merely explained my options. I only have myself to blame, and I do, every day. But you must understand my position"

"Is it done Jacobs?" Ingram suddenly asked Lawrence

"It is, Sir Donald. Thomas, I'm so sorry. I had no choice"

"Oh, please Jacobs stop your whimpering. Here, sit with your friend, he may need your comfort soon, more than he knows"

Ingram stood and replacing his hat looked down at me.

"You were warned Weston, many, many times. You cannot say you were not warned"

"What? What are you saying? I'm sacked?"

Ingram laughed heartily.

"Sacked? Yes, obviously you are sacked. But do you think that being sacked from your employment is your main concern today? You need to think again Mr Weston"

And with that Ingram walked out of the refectory and it was a long time before I saw him again.

*Chapter Thirteen*

Ingram left and with that Lawrence burst into tears. I'd never seen Lawrence so distressed or so distraught in all the years I'd known him and so I moved across the table to hold him while he pulled himself together.

"Thomas, please forgive me, I had no choice, none at all. He would have had me arrested, blamed it all on me. I couldn't go to prison; I wouldn't have survived. Please, you must understand. It was meant only as a warning and if it's really bad you can always find another house"
"Another house? Why would I need another house? I may need another job, but…why? What's happened?"
" Laura was out of the house tonight wasn't she? "
"Yes, for part of the evening, but she came home early…why?"
" And the children were with their grandparent's tonight weren't they? "

He began to look panicked.

"No. They stayed with us for another night - Lawrence, you really must tell me what's happened, why are you so distressed my friend?"

" Oh my God no! Quickly Thomas we must go to your house immediately - before it's too late, my God what have I done? "

"What *have* you done Lawrence? For the last time, what have you done?"

" I paid someone to help me set a small fire at your house - as a warning - nothing more. I'm sure everyone will be alright, but he made me do it Thomas, you must understand"

I ran out into the night and paid an ambulance driver to go as fast as he could and take me back to my house. I couldn't believe what Lawrence had said. Why would he do such a thing, and *who* would do that? As it turned out, the man I thought was my best friend, that was who.

    I know people say 'I'll kill him' in times of anger and stress and never really mean it but I felt anger like I'd never felt before, rising in me - a feeling of such rage that I couldn't breathe let alone give verbal instructions to the driver, instead I waved and pointed at each junction urging him to hurry.

But as we neared my house we came to a sudden halt, the road was filled with carriages and people running with buckets, filled with water I presumed, but I already knew - nothing would save the house, it was half burnt down already and all I could hope for, to pray for was that everyone had got to safety before the fire had fully taken hold.

My hopes were raised when I saw Laura sitting by the back of an ambulance but then the look on her face told me everything I needed to know.

"I couldn't save them Thomas…I tried, I really did, but they were too heavy, and the fire, the smoke, I couldn't see"
"Who…? Who couldn't you save my love - your parents? Was it your parents you couldn't save? Was it your parents that were too heavy?" I daren't ask, but I knew the truth - she meant the children, our Saul and Eloise. But I couldn't see them anywhere and so there was still hope, and guiltily I'd hoped she *had* meant her parents. I looked around for someone who was in charge - a fireman, or a policeman, anyone who might know what had happened and where any survivors were.

"Officer, officer" I called out to a policeman who stood near the house "Please tell me, did the children get out, was there anyone who got out?"

" Got out? No, you must be joking, and if you're from the press, you're a disgrace mate, that's what you are. Some poor sod's lost their family and all you want is a story - it's disgusting "

That told me all I needed to know and as I reeled from this information I tripped over something on the floor. It was a body, covered by a blanket. It was a small blanket and one I recognised as belonging to Eloise. And so that's how I found out my best friend had killed my family. The rage I'd felt earlier returned but I knew I had to look after Laura, I had to be strong for her. I would save Lawrence Jacobs for another day.

The inquest some weeks later pronounced that the four deaths were accidental, even though I told them that Lawrence had set the fire, that he had admitted it to me, and why. I told the court about what had been happening at The Spellbrook, and that I had already been to the police, but no one would listen to me even though I shouted it so loudly I was ejected from the court. That was it, done and dusted. Four lives extinguished and things just moved on - it wasn't right.

The burials were a blur, Laura a ghost by my side. My own life was in ruins but my only thought at that time was for my wife. To lose her parents and her children in one event was incomprehensible and I knew she may never recover from the trauma.

We had to leave England, we had to make a fresh start and though I tried I couldn't find either Lawrence or Ingram to mete out the punishment they deserved. Lawrence may have set the fire, perhaps, as he said as a warning, but that warning had come from Ingram - a man who thought he could do anything to anyone with absolute impunity. Rumours abounded that Ingram had emigrated to America to set up new hospitals and so I believed that my hunt must start there.

Laura hardly spoke but she told me she wanted to go out, by herself and would perhaps stay with a friend for a few days. She said that staying at her parents' house, as we were having to, was too much for her and that she needed to get out, especially before embarking on a lengthy sea journey to America.

And so, my wife stayed with a friend for a few days and I tied up all our financial matters in England. Honestly? I didn't know if we were ever coming back or not - there didn't seem to be anything to come back for.

I knew that I was finished as a surgeon in England - Ingram would have made sure of that and so nothing held me in this country before he left it, but where would he go? Hadn't someone mentioned Boston? Or was that just a rumour - either way it was somewhere to begin.

## *Chapter Fourteen*

James Radcliffe enters the Tewksbury Club and looks around for the man he is due to meet but doesn't see him straight away, not that he knows what he looks like. He takes a seat and is attended to almost immediately by a waiter. Since Sir Donald left England suddenly the Spellbrook needs a new chairman, and James considers that he is that man. He's been told by his fellow surgeon John Whitfield that he would side with him in any vote, and that joining the right club would certainly boost his chances of being in charge at the Spellbrook, if only until Sir Donald returned.

"Can I offer you a drink Sir?" the waiter asks
"Thank you, yes, a whiskey please"
"Certainly Sir, any particular type?"
"I don't know. You decide for me - something smooth, a single malt perhaps"
"Of course. I will be just a moment"

The waiter nods his head in almost a reverential bow and turns towards the bar - Radcliffe can almost taste the whiskey.

He could get used to this - it makes such a change from his usual daily life. He works hard at The Spellbrook, and has people who assist him, but no one who actually waits on him, attends to his every wish, like the members at this wonderful club have. He doesn't earn enough - as his wife regularly reminds him, and so has no servants at home either, and doesn't know what it's like to be waited on, but he knows he could get used to it.

He's been introduced to the man he is due to meet by John Whitfield and, if things go well tonight it's possible he will be invited to join the club. But if he became a member here he could then be waited on any time he wanted. But he is in two minds whether he wants to become a member here. On the one hand there is the obvious prestige that goes with it, the opportunity to mix in the right circles, to 'get on' socially and climb the ladder, and climbing the ladder would mean more money. But on the other hand, the club is very exclusive and therefore very expensive, and on his current salary he would struggle and it's not the sort of thing Mrs Radcliffe would approve of - no, he'd have to…

"Mr Radcliffe?" the waiter asks as he stands tray in hand, whiskey temptingly on the silver platter, only inches away from Radcliffe's nose. He can smell the malt and longs for its warmth on this cold wintery night.

"Thank you. Set it on the table please" Radcliffe tells the waiter
"Sir, if you would follow me, your host has arrived and has asked to meet you in his private room"
"Private room? What's a private room?"
"Somewhere where private matters may be discussed I would presume Sir. They're very popular here at The Tewksbury. If you would follow me, Sir?"

Radcliffe stands and follows the waiter, and his whiskey, along a corridor and waits while the waiter knocks on a door and…also waits.

"Enter" is heard from within.

The waiter opens the door and stands back, allowing Radcliffe to go before him.
Radcliffe walks forward and sees a man and a woman. He doesn't recognise either person and pauses at the door. He turns to see the waiter behind him.

"Please, Sir. Do go in, your whiskey will follow you, never fear"

"Thank you...?"

" Critchley Sir. My name is Critchley, and thank you for asking. I will be just outside if you need anything. Your Lordship. Your Ladyship, Sir" the waiter retreats and closes the door behind him.

Radcliffe stands now, half way between the door and his whiskey, which the waiter - Critchley, set on a table for him. He doesn't know what he's supposed to do, does he bow to the man first, or the woman, or both at the same time. He tries that and it seems to work. The man, Albert, Lord Brunswick steps forward and extends his hand.

" Good evening Radcliffe I am Brunswick, Albert though, please call me Albert"

"I couldn't possibly Sir, Your Lordship, I've only just met you, it would be improper"

"Nonsense, now take a seat Mr Radcliffe...or?"

" James" Radcliffe offers "please do call me James"

"Very well. And if she will excuse my rudeness, James I would like to introduce Elizabeth, who is a lady, though not titled"

"Good evening madam" Radcliffe says and extends his hand

"Good evening Mr Radcliffe" Elizabeth says as she takes the proffered hand " Goodness, what soft hands you have. What do you do for work Mr Radcliffe? May I ask? "

"I am a surgeon; I work at The Spellbrook hospital. Perhaps you know it?"

" Oh yes, I know it, I have been there many times, a wonderful hospital, just wonderful. And how long have you been a surgeon Mr Radcliffe?"

"Oh, some years now, fifteen more or less. One forgets exactly after a while"

Radcliffe takes a sip of his whiskey, and feels the warmth he was expecting, an excellent single malt but he cannot place its origin, an unusual aftertaste, but not unpleasant.

    An hour or so later, and a few more whiskeys later, Radcliffe finds himself gently but firmly being placed in a carriage. He finds himself seated between the man and the woman, but he has no idea how he got here. He does recognise both of the people sitting next to him from earlier, but he is asleep within minutes of the carriage setting off.

As he drifts off he thinks - what a lovely evening he's had, what lovely people they are at The Tewksbury - he really must shake Whitfield's hand, and thank him when he sees him, he isn't a bad chap really.

## *Chapter Fifteen*

As he wakes the first thing he senses is the cold, and as he rouses himself and takes deep, lung filling breaths he sees puffs of freezing air escape from his mouth as he exhales. It feels more like winter down here, dark and dank, for he senses he *is* underground, but he knows everywhere else, outside, it must be daylight by now, and it should be warmer.

His hands are tightly bound behind his back but he manages to get them in front of him but he cannot undo the knots that lash his hands together, they have been expertly tied.

It's damp beneath him and as he puts his hands on the ground and tries to sit up, the overpowering sense now is smell. There is a rotting, decaying odour coming from beneath him and he tries not to breathe it in too deeply, to inhale the rancid, all-pervading smell. It's almost like something, or someone has been here before him and not survived.

He fought in the last war and knows the smell of death, and the cloying taste it leaves in the mouth, but what is this place he thinks? He cannot remember coming here.

He most definitely didn't tie his own hands together and so he tries to think of who would have brought him here, and more importantly, why?

He owes money to people, everyone does, but gambling debts were just that - debts, which would be cleared with the next win, the next fortunate spin of a wheel or turn of a card. No, his debts wouldn't bring him here, people knew him well and knew he could cover them. Someone else then, but who?

He tries to think what his last memory was before coming here, but his head is heavy and his thoughts feel scrambled, as though he's been drugged. Try as he may he cannot think where he was before now, but for some reason the face of Albert, Lord Brunswick swims into his mind. What a strange thought to suddenly have he thinks, what on earth would make him think of Albert.

Had he met him, gone somewhere with him, taken something with him…? But no, he couldn't imagine it, he couldn't imagine such a person doing him harm, why would he? He'd only just met him.

He, and the woman, yes, there had been a woman, and they both seemed so pleasant...

There is a little light coming into the room and so in the gloom he can see a door in front of him and as he becomes used to his surroundings he sees that there is a bed of sorts to his right and a bucket, from which more putrid smells emanate. This has all the makings of a cell - is he in a prison, and if so, what for? He hasn't done anyone any harm. He is a man of medicine, it's not in his nature to harm people. Admittedly there are a few operations at the Spellbrook that he's not proud of...but they don't count...

James Radcliffe stands but as he does he trips and as he stumbles he realises that there is someone else in the room with him.

"Hello?" He quietly calls out into the dark. "Hello? Who are you? Are you alright? "

There is no reply from the shape on the floor, so he calls again as he kneels down

"Hello? Can you hear me? Please.
Say something, anything."

The shape stirs, slowly at first and then scrambles to its feet and stumbles backwards against the wall. It screams, and the sound that comes from the shape is like nothing James has ever heard before. It sounds like a wounded animal caught in a trap, and the sound rings in his ears, but he can't cover them with his tied hands.

"GET OUT!" The shape screams " Get out if you can, before they come. If they come, now there are two of us, God help us! "

James staggers back, the shape shouting at him and the agony contained in the voice shocks him. But there is something in it he recognises, though surely no one he knows?

"Whitfield? Whitfield, is that you?" The man peers into the darkness. "My God, what's happened to you?"

The shape peers back at the man and suddenly begins to weep - this sound worse than the screaming James heard before.

"We are doomed. Radcliffe, if that is you, we are doomed"

"It is Radcliffe, Whitfield, but why? Why are we doomed? We're certainly in a bit of a tight spot, but we're intelligent men, surely we can work things out to get out of here, now there are two of us. Here, untie me and then let's find a way out"

The shape steps back into the dark, where he cannot be seen.

"I cannot untie you Radcliffe" the shape sobs
"Come Whitfield, don't waste time, we may have precious little of it as it is. Here untie my hands"
"I cannot Radcliffe, I have nothing to untie them with" the shape says as he steps out of the gloom.

Radcliffe looks at his former colleague at the Spellbrook Hospital and realises that he cannot help him, for John Whitfield no longer has any hands.

## *Chapter Sixteen*

Samuel Mortenson sits in his kitchen on a wonderful sunlit Sunday morning. He sits with his breakfast laid out before him and a newspaper, freshly delivered and awaiting his attention. His housekeeper came in, made him breakfast and then politely left. He could make his own coffee, he wasn't totally reliant on others, he had a pair of hands for goodness' sake.

Mortenson was a 'bachelor' of sorts, and had no intentions of getting married. Why would he want to give away half his hard-earned income? Why would he want to have to do what another person wanted him to do? He had enough of that at work and now, with Weston being suspended there was even more work for everyone.

It was also particularly galling to Mortenson that having had his holiday request denied by Sir Donald he then allowed two other surgeons to be away at the same time - apparently because a joint venture between Radcliffe and Whitfield had hit the rocks and they were both needed overseas to resolve it, and they hadn't even had the decency to ask personally, or apologise to the remaining staff, just send a telegram and disappear.

Hence it was just him, Jacobs and the old man, and when he was there the old man just got in the way anyway - he was useless, past his prime without doubt and he wouldn't stop interfering. Ingram was also more reliant than ever on the transplant operations keeping the hospital running and so having worked a full day Mortenson was also having to operate in the night just to pay for Ingram's lifestyle - honestly, his hands were worn out and he felt like they might drop off at any minute.

A knock on the door interrupted Mortenson's train of thought, though probably for the best he felt, there was little he could do about things as they stood - Ingram had a hold over him - like the others, and so he best just let it go and make the most of it, and make as much money as he could.

A pleasant enough looking woman stood on the door and introduced herself to Mortenson "Good morning Sir, I'm Elizabeth, may I come in?"

"Why? I'm sorry, do I know you? I was just having my breakfast - it really isn't convenient madam"

"Oh, that is a shame. Shall I call at the hospital later, perhaps speak to your secretary and make an appointment. I think what we need to discuss should be done in private though, don't you? What with everything that's been going on?"

"I have no idea what you're talking about - are you sure you wish to come into my house alone dear lady - it's not seemly"

A voice from behind the woman entered the conversation

"Mr Mortenson, the 'dear lady' is not alone - she is taking a walk with me. Allow me to introduce myself - I am Lord Albert Brunswick, son of the Duke of Brunswick. I assure you Elizabeth has only the best intentions for all concerned"

At this, a more formal, and imposing person on his doorstep, Mortenson stood back and asked both people to enter his home.

"I'm sorry, yes, by all means please go through to the parlour, I will join you in just a moment" Mortenson said

"Oh no, that is alright Sir, I see you have your breakfast before you, please carry on, you never know when you'll be able to eat again do you?" said Elizabeth

"...no...quite. Well, if you don't mind, can I tempt you to anything - I can get a message to my housekeeper?"

"No, that is quite alright, please, sit. May I pour us a coffee though, it has been quite a walk here" Albert said

"Please do, help yourself" Mortenson nodded towards the pot and began to eat his breakfast.

As Albert sat opposite Mortenson, Elizabeth poured them both a coffee from a pot on the kitchen surface behind him.

"May I ask you a question Mr Mortenson?"
"Certainly Your Lordship, anything"
"Do you know Edmund Stanley?"
"...erm...no...I don't think so, should I?"
"No, perhaps not. You should, but perhaps you did not know his name, but you have met him"

"Your Lordship, I see all manner of people in my line of work. I am a surgeon at the Spellbrook Hospital - do you know it? I see many, many people and I'm sorry, I couldn't tell you their names. They appear before me, I operate on them and move on to the next, names don't really matter - they're not really 'people' are they? They are, if you don't mind me saying '10.30 appendix removal' or '11.00 spleen removal' aren't they?"

"Or, perhaps '2.30 in the morning eye removal', now do you remember my brother's name? Think carefully, Sir"

"Ah. I can explain…I assure you; it was necessary…I was told, I only did what I was told to do…"

An extremely sharp knife suddenly appeared at Mortenson's throat and without spilling anyone's coffee Elizabeth placed a pen and paper before him.

"Go ahead then. Please explain in writing what happened. Are you left or right-handed?"

"Right - well, I need both of them, obviously, but I write with the right…"

"Oh, that's good, then please do. Another coffee Albert?"

"No. I'm fine thank you Elizabeth"

"You won't get away with this you know - I know people in high places - Sir Donald Ingram for one - he won't let this go - I assure you"

"Ah, Mr Mortenson, your days as a surgeon are over. There will be no more Sir Donald, and no more Spellbrook - I assure you - now write" Albert said

Ten minutes later Mortenson looked up, sweat pouring down his face

"There. Now get out of my kitchen, get out of my house - you have what you want"

"Oh no Sir - you are coming with us. We have your confession to murder, and surely you see we cannot let that stand. You will have to face the consequences of your actions - we all do at some stage or other, don't you agree? Do you need a coat Sir, it's a little chilly this morning" Elizabeth was all politeness

"You cannot make me come with you - I will not be…" at which point Albert, having heard enough leant across the table, and punched Mortenson clean off his chair. He fell to the kitchen floor, sausage and what may have been egg landing on his waistcoat. But he couldn't eat it, now because he was unconscious, and later..? Well, later he may not be in a position to.

"Rope. We need some rope Elizabeth - I will look in the garden"

Between the two of them Albert and Elizabeth tied Mortenson's arms behind his back and when a knock at the back door came, they loaded him into the waiting carriage, driven by someone who looked suspiciously like a waiter at The Tewksbury.

When they arrive at the house in the country - Albert's getaway house, there is a fresh breeze in the air. On a good day this would be a wonderful thing, it would bring wonderful scents from the forest - of pine and of lavender. But today, close to the barn there are smells that are not quite so fresh, not quite so spring-like and so the three work quickly.

As they enter the barn the two men inside hide from the light that shines in when the hatch in the floor is opened. They cannot hide their eyes with their hands, as they have none and they almost seem to wrestle as they fight for the darkness. They would scream and shout at each other, but they have no tongues - but no one wants to hear what they have to say now anyway. They had their opportunity to say the right things, and they chose not to.

They chose instead to remain silent, and so, for the rest of their lives they will always be silent, until they choose to end things themselves. The stench in here is appalling, but nowhere near as bad as being underground at The Spellbrook was.

Here there is light, here there is food and water and people who will help them. Elizabeth has offered to help them when she has come to visit them. Each has signed a confession, blaming everyone else, and never taking any personal responsibility for their own actions. Having written their lies, their sorry tales of woe, their hands were removed as they wouldn't need them anymore. And as they chose to be a body of one they were bound together, professionally of course - advanced needlework and years of tapestry when she was an unofficial seamstress has gained Elizabeth a multitude of skills. It was messy at first, but after the third one, hands were not a real problem - so long as the cut was clean and the wound was dressed properly there was never too much infection, not that these surgeons ever worried about that when *they* removed limbs.

Having prepared him properly Mortenson is joined to the others and left to wake up and perhaps regret not having finished his breakfast while he could, without someone having to help him.

## *Chapter Seventeen*

It was some days after the fire at Thomas's house and Lawrence sat alone in the hospital gardens, head in hands.

He hadn't slept since that day, and couldn't since, even when he tried, for all he could see were the people burning.

He hadn't stayed at the fire once it had taken hold. He'd told the person who'd helped him to go, and leave it to him.

It *was* only meant as a warning to Thomas, but once the fire truly started he knew he couldn't stop it. He honestly believed no-one was in the house, and he continued to believe that until he heard the first screams coming from upstairs. And that was when he froze - he was residing at the house off and on, so he could easily explain his presence there, but being fully dressed, in the dead of night, and outside, not inside, helping the screaming, burning occupants? And so, he had just stood there.

Why had he done it? Why had he thought this was the right thing to do? Why hadn't he stood up to Ingram - this was his lifelong friend…and he was setting light to his house? What on earth had made him do this?

Ingram warned Lawrence that his friend should be very careful what he was doing and saying when he was at the hospital. He'd told him to speak to Thomas and warn him not to go up against him, or 'his friends', and in the meantime he would look for a way to remove Thomas from The Spellbrook with no awkward questions being raised, perhaps even get him employment elsewhere, or at least a decent reference.

The hospital owner also had told him to advise his friend that there would be no more warnings, either he toed the line or he would be made to pay. And Lawrence had tried, he'd told Thomas he needed to be careful, to keep his head down and just do the work, or leave - either way, not to go up against Sir Donald Ingram.

And so, he'd been told to set the fire - as a last warning, but then he'd heard the screams…and eventually he'd run, as fast as he could, to the only place he could think of going - The Spellbrook.

There he'd met Ingram, and at first told him he hadn't been able to do it - to set the fire. But Ingram had reminded him of his position, and his options. He had two choices - one - do what he was told, or two - be handed over to the police with all the evidence of what he, and he alone had been doing to and with the new patients, including the birth certificates of children he'd fathered.

  And so, Lawrence told Ingram what *had* happened, what he *had* done, and rode with him to The Hampton where he was told to pull himself together as he may be needed soon to console his friend. En route, Ingram reminded Lawrence that the fire was only meant as a warning and that if anyone died in it then that would definitely be between him and his conscience, as he himself had been at his club when the unfortunate event had apparently occurred and had any number of witnesses should they be needed.

  Lawrence knew that Ingram would walk away from this, he would use his position and his wealth to come out of 'this terrible tragedy' totally blamelessly, whilst letting him take the fall if need be. He couldn't stay in London, he had to get away, but he had nowhere to go and now he was truly alone.

As far as he knew Ingram had abandoned ship and gone who knew where, whilst Radcliffe and Whitfield were still overseas trying to save some business venture or other, with no known return date. And Thomas and Laura?

As he sat in the hospital gardens he thought back to Laura. This was where he'd first met her - the beautiful woman with the sunglasses. She used to sit on this very bench, usually with a nurse and do her needlework. He used to deliberately take his lunch here when he thought there was the best chance of seeing her - but he'd been too afraid to approach her, let alone speak to her, and so he stood, pretending to read a book he held in his hands, whilst watching hers - delicate and slim.

He had watched her for a number of weeks before he finally did go to her, but it was not in a sunlit garden that he made his move, no flowers picked from those around her. One night he had ensured that the other people in her room were asleep, by drugging them and putting them back in their almost comatose state before approaching her. He was not proud of what happened that night and subsequently, but he was just a man and he had needs. This woman though strapped to a bed, night after night and almost drugged into oblivion was the most beautiful thing he had ever seen and he had to have her.

He didn't know why she was here, or what the matter with her was, and to be honest he didn't really care. Lawrence continued his nightly visits to the woman, but stopped taking his lunch in the gardens. In the day he was too ashamed of what he had done repeatedly to her during the night to view her in the sunlight, but he was addicted and so returned again and again - he had been honest with Thomas when he'd said he was addicted, but it wasn't to gambling - and now? Now, Thomas had married the woman, he had done the decent thing when she had become pregnant, twice.

    Lawrence knew that at least one child must have been his - the eldest one whom she had called Eloise, but he was not certain about the boy - Saul, he didn't think he had been his, but knew that he hadn't been Thomas's child either as he had confided in his friend that they had found it was not possible for them to have children..

    Lawrence returned to the only place he knew - The Spellbrook - he felt he should book himself into the ward downstairs and have done with it, just drift away in a drugged haze - he was a coward, he knew it. He should end things here and now, but he didn't have the nerve to do it and so he sat, in the gardens, almost totally alone.

## *Chapter Eighteen*

While Laura stayed with an unnamed friend I tied up all the financial loose ends that I could. I knew it was time for us to move on and to make a fresh start. We had nothing left to keep us in London and as I'd said to Lawrence a new challenge was what I personally needed. Ingram wouldn't let me practise as a surgeon in London and who knew how far his reach within medicine was, but I felt if I stayed in the profession somehow, I may find out where he'd gone and track him down.

The house we'd lived in happily I thought, for some years was no more, but an insurance company told me there was an investigation taking place into the circumstances of the fire burning it to the ground. And so there should be, I told them, for it was no accident. Though by saying what I did I may have brought what subsequently happened to me upon myself, as a few days later there was a knock on the front door, *our* front door I supposed, as we had taken to staying at Laura's parent's house.

"Good morning, may I help you?"

" Mr Weston? "

"Yes?"

"Mr Thomas Weston?"

" Yes? "

"Is this your house Sir?"

"No"

"Then may I ask what you're doing here?"

"I live here"

"I thought you said it's not your house?"

"It isn't my house, it belongs, belonged, to my wife's parents"

"Your wife's dead parents?"

"Yes…sorry who are you?"

"I am Detective Inspector Fotheringham, of the City of London police force" as he produced his warrant card.

"Oh? And how can I help you this morning, Detective Inspector? "

"I need you to come with me to answer some questions"

"Very well. I'm glad you've called as I have some questions of my own" I said

We adjourned to the police station and I was interviewed regarding the fire which I was pleased about. I told the policeman that I knew that the fire had been started deliberately and that Lawrence Jacobs was the man they should be speaking to, and arresting for the murders of our children and Laura's parents.

Fotheringham pointed out that the coroner's court had ruled that the fire was an accident and thus the deaths were not murders, but accidental deaths. In any event he said, he could not locate Lawrence but had left word for him at The Spellbrook.

Fotheringham paused, but then said

"Now Mr Weston. To business, the real reason I brought you here.."
" Wait a moment...I've just told you that the 'accident' you, and everyone else seems so eager to sweep under the carpet, was the murder of four innocent people. I've told you who did it and you've what..? You've 'left a message' for the murderer? Good God man, have some sense! "
"Now then sir, I appreciate you're somewhat upset at the moment, but I'd ask you to calm down."

"Somewhat upset? My children have been murdered; my in-laws have been murdered...! A bit upset?"

"Mr Weston, what do you think of James Radcliffe?"

"Radcliffe? He's alright I suppose. A decent enough man, a good surgeon"

"Not anymore he's not"

"Sorry"

"I said, not anymore he's not"

"Why? I don't understand?"

"And Whitfield - John Whitfield?"

"Again, a decent enough surgeon - look, what's this about, why are you asking me about my colleagues?"

"Your former colleagues"

"Well yes, my former colleagues"

"And Samuel Mortenson? What do you think about him - a decent surgeon as well?

"Yes, I suppose so - sorry, why are you asking me all of this - has something happened to them?"

"Oh, why do you ask that sir?"

"Well...I presumed..."

"Yes?"

"I don't know, look, I would like to leave"

"I bet you would Mr Weston, sit down please."

"Unless you're going to arrest me Inspector then I will be leaving."

Not a good thing to say to a Detective Inspector as I was then arrested for the murders of my three former colleagues. I was informed that they had been found dead a couple of mornings ago, but it was the circumstances in which they were found that had me hurriedly grabbing a waste paper bin and being violently sick into it.

Fotheringham then told me that the three men, whom I had accused, along with Sir Donald of operating on hundreds of long-term patients, had been found with their wrists and legs sewn together, apparently quite professionally; and their tongues had also been removed, again quite expertly. I was told that they had been found underground, beneath a barn on land belonging to the Duke of Brunswick, and then I was asked if I knew him. I could see that this looked very bad for me - I was a surgeon after all.

"Sorry Inspector, you're asking me if I know the Duke of Brunswick?"
"Yes, I am"
"No, I do not know him or any of his family"
"And why do you think they were sewn together?"

"How the hell would I know that? You've only just told me about it, I've not had time to form an opinion, or even a guess"

"Now, I understand at the inquest into the deaths of...the deaths, you accused these men..."

"Yes I accused them..."

"You also accused Sir Donald Ingram, didn't you Mr Weston?"

"Yes, I accused Ingram...and the others of systematic abuse of patients at The Spellbrook...and probably murder, not that you'd be interested in that I wouldn't suppose"

"You weren't so unsure at the inquest Mr Weston, you said definitely murder"

"No...I was...my children...surely you don't think?"

"So, Mr Weston - who do you know who had a grudge against these men"

"I've no idea Inspector, none at all"

"Did you?"

"Did I what?"

"Did you have a grudge against them at all?"

"No"

"Are you sure? Hadn't you just been sacked by Sir Donald? Hadn't he prevented you from continuing a very wealthy life as a surgeon?"

"Yes, that's true, but he hasn't been found with his hands cut off has he? Or has he? And I didn't have a grudge against the other three. And even if I did have a grudge against them, why in God's name would I cut their hands off, that's horrible, that's barbaric"

"I didn't say that their hands had been removed, Mr Weston".

"You said that they were sewn together by their wrists"

"I did"

"And to do that you'd have to remove their hands, wouldn't you?"

"Well Sir, I'll take your word for it, you are the surgeon here, not me. Now then Sir, one last question and then you can be on your way"

"Certainly"

"Where *is* Sir Donald Ingram?"

I was stunned. I couldn't believe what was happening. The fire had been hushed up at the time by Ingram as an accident, but now? Someone had brutally slain my three colleagues and Ingram and Lawrence had disappeared, which seemingly left only me to carry the can for everything that had happened. I knew what this looked like, but I am a good person, honestly.

I've never knowingly done any harm to anyone, but if it wasn't Ingram or Lawrence, then who was it? I was allowed to leave the police station but was told that I had to remain in contact and be available for any further interview.

I knew that this looked very bad for me, and whilst I knew what it would look like, it only hastened my need to leave the city. I knew that Ingram would still be alive - he had just vanished, he had rid himself of this little inconvenience and moved on, to make a fresh start, as I also felt I must, but where would he go?

## Chapter Nineteen

And so, we did travel to America - we had to, as no one I knew within the medical profession knew where Ingram had gone. All I had left was the rumour that he'd emigrated, and so I followed it. I'd seen how large a country America was, but I had to start somewhere. I had to at least try to track down the man responsible for ruining my life and that of my wife. I had tried to continue as a surgeon, but as I suspected he would, Ingram had blocked me doing that, even here - and whilst no one knew where he was, his word was everywhere 'do not employ Weston'.

I was finished as a surgeon and so for the next two years I studied a version of doctoring called psychology, which was reasonably new and a very rough type of subject in all honesty. I had always felt, as you know, that the physical body was what we professionals should look after first and the mind would follow; but this branch of medicine reversed that thinking.

It professed that if the mind was right then the body would follow and that the mind could be trained effectively to help the body heal - as I say it was a very new subject, but as it transpired one that many people were willing to try and to pay me handsomely for listening to them.

Over the next two years I studied psychology and had taken up a number of short-term positions in various hospitals in America, which suited me as it allowed me the cover of moving on when I didn't find Ingram. It wasn't as easy as asking did anyone know of an Englishman who used to be called Sir Donald Ingram and may or may not be running a hospital somewhere in America, and so we found ourselves moving many times and starting again, in a new house, in a new city, but throughout everything we stayed together. Each time we'd moved I felt, this was it, we would find Ingram in this city; but each time I was mistaken, and each time I was disappointed in our choice, and in the outcome, both for myself and for my wife.

Laura hadn't minded moving from city to city, she'd said so many times that she'd always wanted to travel and this was her way of appeasing me I suppose, accepting that we needed to move on, we needed to gather our things once more and try again she had said, another job, another city and there were plenty to choose from in this vast country - a man could easily get lost just trying to find himself.

This particular choice, this new 'adventure' as Laura would have described it in better times, was to be in Boston and my new first day started early. When we'd left England it had been my intention to go straight to Boston and look for Ingram, but I had no proof of what had happened at the Spellbrook and could not find him at any hospital in that city in any event. We needed money to survive and hence I had been working at my new profession for some time but Boston kept nagging at me and so we came to the city at last, and it was by a long-winded process that I hoped I had found who I was looking for.

I was due at the hospital at eight o'clock to meet the President - Sir Philip Upton, an Englishman who had apparently emigrated to the United States some five years ago, perhaps for his own new start, his own adventure, and who ran the establishment I was on my way to, along his own strict lines, which included deference and subservience to him in all things, if I was to believe what I had heard. He sounded so like Sir Donald that my hopes were raised, but I hadn't met the man who was to be my new boss if things went well, and so I tried to contain my enthusiasm.

As I made my way up the hill towards the St. Francis Hospital - known locally as Frankie's, I will admit I was somewhat apprehensive as to what awaited me there, perhaps my search was over, but what would I do if it was? How would I 'mete out justice?'

I had written to a number of Boston hospitals but had heard back from just this one, from a man called William Stanwick, who perhaps a little pompously had introduced himself as the 'Secretary to the President'.

    The day was cold and overcast and with the threat of rain I had donned my great coat and gloves, and as I approached the imposing gates of the institution I was sweating profusely. I slowed my pace, removed my gloves and stood looking at the building where I was to spend just the next two months of my life, although obviously I did not know that at the time.

    I was met at the door by a porter who led me towards Stanwick's office and, showing me to a waiting area outside, offered me a seat and advised me he would be just a moment whilst he located Sir Philip's assistant.

I had been waiting for about ten minutes when, on the stroke of eight o'clock a door opened and a short, stout man appeared.

"Mr Weston?" He enquired
" Yes. Good morning Sir, I am Thomas Weston " I replied.
" Come through please. I am William Stanwick, Secretary to Sir Philip Upton" the man confirmed and with a wave of his arm showed me into his office. I collected my hat and gloves and entered the room, with Stanwick following me.

He walked past me and sat at a large desk in the centre of the room, leaving me standing just inside the door.

Thinking this was perhaps a test of some sort, I closed the door, removed my coat and hung it on the hatstand just inside the room, placing my hat and gloves on a nearby table.

I approached the desk and feeling a little like a pupil before a master, I awaited permission to sit before him. It was duly granted and I took my place in an adequately comfortable seat in front of the desk.

"So, Mr Weston, I have read your application letter and you seem well qualified, but, if I may say, also well-travelled?"

"Yes, Sir…"

" I am not a Sir, I am a Mr. As are you, Mr Weston. It is Sir Philip who is the Sir, not I"

"Oh, I am sorry, I was being polite Mr Stanwick, I do apologise"

" No need Mr Weston, but just so you know."

"Indeed…yes, I am well-travelled, as you say. I have been at a number of hospitals and have gained much valuable experience in the field in which I now specialise. "

"Psychology? Is that what you call it?" He said with what appeared to be a disdainful sneer.

" Yes psychology, that's what it's called - the study of the mind - a fascinating area of medicine and one which will, in years to come…"

"Well travelled though?"

" Experienced though. I was a surgeon for many years"

"We will see…Mr Weston. Now references? Do you have them with you, or must I send off for them, which would be most inconvenient, and would unnecessarily delay things"

Conveniently, for me at least I had three references from previous hospitals I had attended, all written in a wonderful hand, perhaps that of a most competent secretary, or perhaps not. I passed the references to Stanwick and inwardly wished him well in tracking down their senders.

"Are we waiting for Sir Philip, Mr Stanwick?" I asked
"Waiting?"
"Yes...for Sir Philip?"
"You? Waiting? For Sir Philip?"
"Yes. To speak with him?"
"Why no, Mr Weston. We are not waiting for Sir Philip. You are unlikely ever to meet Sir Philip, let alone speak with him, no, no. You will not be meeting Sir Philip, he travels, I understand he is currently abroad. This is your meeting with me, and we are finished."
"Finished, Mr Stanwick? I've only been here a few minutes"
"You have. And I will let you know our decision. Unless you have any questions?"

I should have had so many questions, concerning salary, working times and conditions, what staff I would have under me and so on, but I had the impression that I wouldn't be hearing from Mr Stanwick anytime soon, and so I stood, and thanked him for his time. The one question I should have asked the pompous little man though was - do you have a picture of Sir Phillip?

## *Chapter Twenty*

I left the hospital not knowing where I was going. I could wander around the city, use up some time, make it seem when I arrived home that I'd had a full-length, in-depth interview with a board of esteemed doctors, followed by a tour of the facilities and lunch with Sir Philip and that he was in fact Sir Donald Ingram.

Or I could return to our rooms and tell Laura the truth.

I had been seen by the understudy, corrected and sneered at, and then dismissed like a lacky, no longer needed or considered necessary - 'I will let you know our decision!' - like he was important, like he mattered, and would be part of the process. I knew I wasn't a doctor here, merely a 'Mr', as 'Mr' Stanwick had so clearly pointed out, whilst not actually saying, I was beneath him.

I would tell Laura the truth, as I always would, no matter the consequences - we would always be together and so there was no risk in being honest with her, not really. It did her no harm.
Any harm I had inflicted upon her had been done a long time ago, and yet she had stayed with me.

    I had been at a number of hospitals and worked my way through all manner of patients and departments, but this one, this opportunity if it came, would be like no other, I could feel it, and I couldn't wait to tell Laura about it. I thought we *had* found him, Ingram. How ironic that with us having come this far he was possibly back in England, safe and sound under an assumed name - it must be him; the odds were too impossible for it not to be.

    When I got back it was quiet, and the stillness was calming. I preferred the silence, the not having to explain myself, that would come later I was sure. Laura was there in our room at a small hotel near the railway station, and she seemed calm and relaxed, and so I didn't try to wake her.

    The landlady had been very understanding when we arrived a few days ago to take up rooms at her boarding house.

I had initially looked at them by myself, as I thought that would be more convenient, and easier for everyone under the circumstances, but it had been, shall we say, awkward.

"Good day Mr Weston, nice to meet you at last" Mrs Ogilvy, the prospective landlady had said when she greeted me at the door.
"And a good day to you too Mrs Ogilvy. I do apologise, and hope I'm not too late...the trains...I...we..."
"No. No. Not late at all, is Mrs Weston still in the carriage...I take it there is a Mrs Weston...?"
"Oh yes, there is a Mrs Weston, though I've had to leave her at the station hotel, she was...tired after the journey..."
"Yes indeed, well you've come all the way from England, a long voyage, and so suddenly, I understand, very mysterious!" I'd said that we had come directly to Boston so as to avoid any unnecessary or troublesome questions about where else we'd stayed and why for such short periods of time.
"Ah, there is no mystery I assure you, my wife has been...unwell, for quite some time and we have come to America for...alternative treatments to the type she was receiving in England, that's all"

"She *will* be joining you though Mr Weston won't she? I can't have a single gentleman under my roof, I already have a number of single ladies…and…well, I'm sure you understand?"
"Oh yes, she'll be joining me. If I may see the rooms and perhaps have a little supper, and in the morning I will return to the station and collect Mrs Weston, if that would be acceptable?"
"Certainly Mr Weston, please go through to the drawing room. I'll bring you some tea."

Whilst the landlady headed for the kitchen I turned right off the narrow hallway and entered the drawing room, a space much larger than I'd expected of the small house. There were a few large and comfortable looking armchairs placed loosely in a semi-circle near the fireplace and it seemed as if only moments ago they'd been occupied, there were a number of cups on side tables, some of which still held tea, and were warm to the touch. I removed my hand from a tea cup as the door opened and Mrs Ogilvy entered with a tray.

"Ah, please excuse the untidiness Mr. Weston, let me clear these things away"
"Oh, it's no trouble Mrs Ogilvy, have I interrupted something, it looks like I have?"

"No, not interrupted, just brought things to a close Mr Weston. My ladies and I were, well, if I'm honest, we were discussing you!"

" Me? Why would you be discussing me? There's not much to discuss I assure you Mrs Ogilvy"

"Well, I've been showing the ladies the newspaper cuttings, from England, and your…situation there."

" Yes. Well. That is all behind me now, I assure you, all in the dim and distant past, and not for a social circle to pore over with tea and cakes surely? "

"Oh, the ladies were just interested, Mr Weston, it's like we were to have our own famous person under our roof, and they were excited, and keen to meet you, perhaps tomorrow, with Mrs Weston obviously, once you're both settled, perhaps in the afternoon?"

"I'm happy to meet 'the ladies', and to dispel any rumour or uncertainty that exists about my past, my distant past, or my 'infamy' Mrs Ogilvy, but it's not something that I would put my wife through, she's suffered enough, and…well, I am sure you can imagine?"

"Oh, no, I didn't mean, I was only…"

"It's quite alright Mrs Ogilvy, calm yourself, I take no offence, I have become used to…intrigue, preceding me?"

Mrs Ogilvy busied herself with the tea things and laid out some cold cuts and bread on a plate before me. Having done so she excused herself and left me with the dwindling embers of the fire and my thoughts.

## *Chapter Twenty-One*

The following morning, I dressed and asked the landlady for a small breakfast, Mrs Ogilvy was the only other occupant of the room and as she busied herself with my eggs and bacon I read the local paper. I'd been asked if I'd mind having a later breakfast as 'the ladies' fully took up the room and she needed to ensure they all got off to work on time. I didn't mind as to be honest I was in no great rush to entertain the other guests and so I was happy to await their departure.

Having answered a knock on the door the landlady returned clutching a number of letters to her ample bosom. Holding it out she passed me a letter which looked official in its buff envelope, and felt weighty in its content.

"Oh, the post has arrived - and look there's something for you Mr Weston - who knows you're here though? Officially I mean?" Mrs Ogilvy enquired

"No one Mrs Ogilvy, I assure you, apart from St Francis Hospital? I attended an interview there yesterday, I hope you don't mind, I gave them this address?" I apologised

" Well, there you are then, how exciting!" she said as she handed over an envelope and waited…apparently this was to be a joint opening as she stood close to the edge of my breakfast table.

I opened the envelope and saw to my ultimate surprise that the answers to the questions I should have asked Stanwick were here before me. I was to be employed as a psychologist at St Francis, on a probationary footing initially for three months. My proposed salary and working conditions were laid out in the letter and there was a presumption that I would accept the offer, as it contained an instruction to sign on the dotted line of the last page, and return 'all documents' to Stanwick, which I obviously would. Thanking her for breakfast I excused myself and my private mail from Mrs Ogilvy's close observation and went to our room to write my letter of acceptance.

I hoped that in accepting the position I'd been offered I'd be able to ask questions from within St Francis' and who knew, perhaps one day in those three months even meet my benefactor, and if not then I would at least gain some valuable experience in my new chosen field.

Looking back, I suppose it should have been surprising to me that I was so readily offered employment at St Francis - as I've said the Secretary acting as he had towards me had given me little hope of me landing a job there and I expected a rejection as had often happened recently. However, the field of psychology was a new one and perhaps this hospital wanted to try it out, and maybe develop its use if it brought in patients, and therefore money to them. The fact that the English President may have manufactured me being there in the first place never crossed my mind, nor the fact that things often happened for reasons not of one's choosing but of someone else's making. I had come to Boston searching for my prey, but had I found him, or had he allowed himself to be found, and was just toying with me? Had he gone back to England having rid himself of me once more?

Or was I thinking too deeply about this hospital and presuming the President was Ingram under a different name, when in fact it was just a fellow countryman doing someone a favour?

I left the accommodation and returned to the railway station. It had a modest hotel attached to it and I had taken a room for a couple of nights, where I had managed to lodge my wife alone without too many people seeing her or bothering her unduly.

She had rested well it would seem, but was fairly unresponsive to me when I spoke with her. I told her of our new accommodation, my prospective employment and of the ladies that would like to hear of our troubles, like it was some story from a Victorian Penny Dreadful, but she said little, perhaps the journey had tired her more than she let on.

Laura knew that I had been arrested for the murders of Radcliffe, Whitfield and Mortenson, and yet she never asked me about it, not once. Whenever the matter was raised she just said 'you didn't do it, without hesitation or doubt.

She never doubted *my* honesty towards her, and to think that I had doubted *her* honesty and even questioned her faithfulness to me. She was such an honest woman and I was blessed to have her as my wife.

We didn't speak of the murders any more once we'd left the English shores and that was fine by me - I wanted nothing more to do with the horrors of the Spellbrook and had done what I could before I left, and I knew that my conscience was clear. I'd alerted the authorities to what I suspected had gone on there, but was met with disbelief as Ingram's 'friends' no doubt closed ranks around him, wherever he was. I knew that the police and the hospital board would just let the passage of time wash over the terrible happenings, and that no-one would ever be brought to account for their actions.

I however, did want to bring Ingram to justice and so, if we were to stay in this city until we found him, or could cross it off our list then I suppose we would have to endure a little interest in us, and so I had acquiesced to Mrs Ogilvy's request to speak to 'her ladies' though I was not going to say too much.

## *Chapter Twenty-Two*

It was late afternoon and the 'ladies' were ushered into the sitting room, filing in, looking at both of us in particular, and as they did they whispered behind their hands, I was something of a conundrum to them, something to be stared at and gossiped about - the wife of a murderer I thought heard them think, but they were wrong, Thomas wasn't a murderer, he couldn't be. They wouldn't accuse him outright, but they would suspect all sorts of things about me, just for being married to him.

They nodded and smiled at Thomas, for he was, in his own way, a handsome man, but averted their eyes from me, preferring instead to lower their gaze, find their seats and drink their tea which the landlady had provided for them.

I wanted people to know what had happened, but the whole truth? Even though I didn't know what the whole truth was, I was responsible for some of it. I felt, no I knew that Ingram had come to America - the rumours were that he had many businesses here and it would make sense for him to run to somewhere like this, somewhere safe, but far enough away to remove himself from the scandal at the Spellbrook, and being as wealthy as he was he could live just as well here as he could in England. I'd urged Thomas to bring us here, to try to track Ingram down and make him face justice, for Thomas said we now had proof that Ingram had been involved in terrible things that had been happening at The Spellbrook and his word was good enough for me. If that were the case then Ingram would pay for his crimes, one way or the other, I would make sure of it.

Thomas was a good man - we'd had our share of disagreements and upsets along the way but overall, I'd been pleased with my choice - my second choice admittedly, but even so still my choice. My first choice had been to raise my children myself, without ever having to rely on a man. I'd tried twice to do that and twice my so-called parents had had me sent back to a hospital for my 'own good'. God only knows what would have happened to me if I had stayed at the Spellbrook any longer, once I had outlived my usefulness to the likes of the doctor and the others - I probably would have been used like the other poor souls in that ward.

Whilst Thomas was a good man, the problem with him though was that he believed everything he was told, provided it was told well - with sincerity, and so he had believed me when I had told him my story. Despite what he thought of me I had not been 'unfaithful' to him, not in the true sense of the word. I had not willingly been with another man, although I *had* been with other men - but that certainly was never of my choosing.

    I had had two children by this one other man, and I think you can guess who it was and under what circumstances Saul and Eloise were conceived. Both children had been taken from me immediately after their births as was always the case with people in my circumstances - it happened more often than you could imagine or want to think about. My children were handed to my parents - which was ironic seeing as they would not look after *me*, their own flesh and blood when I was born. Perhaps they felt this was a balancing of the books by looking after them, seeing how they treated me the way they did - sending me away rather than protecting me from the world.

What made me do what I did though was the fact that they never once asked questions, they never asked how someone who had been sent to a hospital for their 'rest and recuperation' could become pregnant, not once but twice.

But my parents were no more, they had died in the fire at our home and I suppose I should have grieved, but all my grief was taken up by the loss of my children and I had felt nothing towards them as what was left of them was buried.

With the ladies now seated and avidly anticipating a show, the landlady Mrs Ogilvy stood in front of Thomas and I. It was as if we were being presented - paraded for their amusement, but Thomas had wanted to speak to them, to let them know that there was nothing they should worry about whilst staying here - we weren't a pair of psychopaths living under their roof, we were just average people, like them. But we knew how gossip could easily spread and we didn't want everyone knowing we were in the city, just in case we did find Ingram.

"Ladies. We have with us Mr and Mrs Thomas Weston, from England. They have come here to start a new life, following what you will have heard were tragic events for them both. I know that we have spoken about them as things were said in the newspapers and all sorts of wild speculations were raised by, well, shall we say the less salubrious versions of the news of the day.

    Mr and Mrs Weston may very well be staying with us for a time and so wanted to put your minds at rest and have said that they are more than willing to answer any questions you may have for them. So, without further ado I will hand you over to Mr Weston."

## *Chapter Twenty-Three*

The introductions being over, Thomas stood, clearly embarrassed, as I knew he would be. He was not one for public speaking and it showed as he wrung his hands together and then settled for putting them behind his back, out of sight.

"Ladies…well, this is…pleasant. It's almost like we're celebrities, but we're not, really, we're not, and so I will sit down again" and Thomas sat. "As Mrs Ogilvy said, we'd like to stay here for some time, settle here in Boston, if you'll have us, indeed I've been offered employment at a local hospital, and so I'm hopeful that we'll be 'seeing you around', as you say here, for some time. And as such we didn't want you to feel uncomfortable in your own home, well Mrs Ogilvy's home…" Thomas paused, but then continued "Ladies. What happened *was*…tragic. We were heartbroken by the deaths of our loved ones and felt a new start, in your fine country was best for us - to get away and try to move on.

There is no mystery to what happened to me, to us, just a set of tragic circumstances that we lived through, nothing more. Now, who would like more tea?"

And that was it. As far as Thomas was concerned he had nothing else to say, other than 'we are who we are' and 'more sugar madam?' the ladies began to chatter between themselves.

I was angry, but being, as far as people viewed me anyway, a genteel English lady with a man to speak for her, was expected to remain silent and smile pleasantly. I didn't think so, and so I stood.

"Laura..?" Thomas nearly spat his tea over me "Thomas" I said in a voice that he knew he should not counter "Ladies, if I may? I would like to say something"

The ladies quietened down and faced me, for the first time that afternoon. I could see that they were shocked, as even here women did not defy their 'menfolk'. Whilst it was the early part of the twentieth century I felt we had been stuck in the dark ages for too long, and well, I had nothing to lose.

"Ladies. I am Laura Weston, my husband Thomas is a polite and kind man, but you need to know the truth, at least as far as we know it. It is true that my husband was employed at the famous Spellbrook Hospital in London - I think you may have heard of it, and he was good at his job. But he would not tell you that - in fact he was brilliant at his job - he was a surgeon and performed many, many lifesaving and life changing operations in his time there. Now, I do not wish to shock you, and I'm sorry if this is too close to home, either now or in the past, but I also…"

"Laura…no!" Thomas interjected

"Thomas…the ladies wish for a little information on which to base their thoughts, and their views of us, and so rather than reading it in the press, I think they should know the truth - don't you?"

"But Laura…"

"Thomas, it's alright. As I was saying ladies, I was also at The Spellbrook for some time…"

"As a nurse? Is that how you met?" one of the ladies asked.

"No. Not as a nurse, but as a patient…"

"Had you had a baby?" another asked.

"I had two children while I was at the hospital, but no. That is not how we met, ladies. I had found myself in difficult circumstances and Thomas rescued me, saved me from a terrible fate – and though you couldn't imagine it, you shouldn't dwell on it, or think too deeply about it. We had a family, two lovely children and a wonderful life together, and for many years we were happy…"

"We heard they were stitched together…" one of the ladies couldn't hold it back any further

"Laverne! For goodness' sake!"

"Well, that's what the papers said…"

"Not the one I read…"

"They had their tongues cut out! That's what I heard"

"Ladies please, let us not descend into conjecture, please let Mrs Weston speak" Mrs Ogilvy pleaded.

"Thank you Mrs Ogilvy" I said "The thing we want you to remember is that three of my husband's colleagues were horribly murdered and his best friend has been missing now for some time. We are heartbroken that someone so close to us may be out there, although he may also be with God, but it is the not knowing that weighs on us so heavily"

"Is that right you were arrested for the murders, Mr Weston?"

"I was yes" Thomas replied "but as you can see I escaped the hangman - it must be my politeness and kindness!" he said, which caused a ripple of polite and kind laughter among those assembled.

"And your boss - Ingram? He didn't help you at all? He must have known you had nothing to do with it surely?" A lady couldn't help herself shouting out

"My boss? My boss did nothing to aid me, or my wife's position, ladies. I fear he saw that he too may have been suspected of foul deeds and so removed himself from the situation…"

"Mr Weston is again, too polite and too kind, ladies". I corrected him "Sir Donald Ingram was the man who pointed the finger of suspicion at Thomas. It was Sir Donald Ingram who had Thomas arrested and were it not for people speaking on Thomas's behalf I am sure he would not be with us today. The knight of the realm then disappeared from the hospital, and England it would seem and has not been seen since".

There was a general consensus that that was not the actions of an English gentleman or indeed an innocent man, which I think we all agreed on, but there you have it, that was what had happened.

    The afternoon continued but Thomas would say no more, and, he reminded me, I had said enough.

## *Chapter Twenty-Four*

It was the man's hands that I first noticed. I had seen them for years, close up, firm but delicate as they worked, sewing, cutting, pointing out to me where to hold, where to pull and where to swab.

I had seen them opposite me for many years with their owners' head bent down, concentrating under poor lighting, sweat pouring from his brow as he worked, often desperately trying to save a life, mostly with success, but sometimes not.

The hands that would point to others giving instructions to nurses to do their bidding, and they were always obeyed, for they were the hands of a master craftsman and they dictated what happened when they were working properly.

I would know those hands anywhere and yet it could not be, they could not be there, sitting at a table not ten yards from me, after all this time, after all this searching.

And yet there they were casually turning the pages of the newspaper without a care in the world.

Their owner sitting in the sunshine, sipping coffee and eating pastries in the mid-morning air, while my wife, my beloved Laura, had laid in the darkness, drifting in and out of wakefulness, and our children and their grandparents had lain in their graves these past few years.

Whether Sir Donald Ingram had noticed me or not I did not know, if he did he gave no sign of it as I watched him. He was not the sort of man to look up, or take notice of what others were doing around him, for his world consisted only of him. The only people I ever saw him interact with were servants to him - waiters, nurses, secretaries and so on, the rest were…beneath him, unnecessary interruptions and distractions in his life.

One of the hands reached out and flicked a crumb from an immaculately pressed trouser leg and then clicked their finger and thumb at a passing waiter.

A small thin man almost ran to Ingram's table and hovered, wringing his own hands together whilst awaiting his instructions from the customer.

With a bark and a point of a long delicate finger Ingram ordered more coffee, and with a vigorous nod of the head the waiter ran back the way he had come and returned with a steaming pot for him.

Ingram waited whilst the coffee was poured and then shooed the waiter away, returning with a flourish to his paper and the last of his pastry.

How could this man sit, without a care in the world, with no worries or concerns in his life, while the others he had trodden upon and left in his wake fretted and agonised each and every day in theirs, myself included.

I had to do something, to end his life, in order to take back mine, for I was sure that Sir Donald Ingram had been responsible for the deaths of my loved ones and I would never be able to live again if I did not make him pay.

But I could not approach him now. If I did, what would I say? 'Ah Sir Donald, a lovely morning is it not?' And see what his reaction was. Or how about 'you killed my family and I thought you had *disappeared*?' No, perhaps not. I knew I must withdraw and replan what I should do. I hadn't envisaged killing him if I found him, for what, revenge, or justice? But now that he was so close I wasn't so sure - he deserved to die certainly, but nothing I would do would bring our children back. There was just me, and what was left of Laura, a shell of a woman, without hope, without purpose, but what was *I* to do?

The man made my decision for me. He rose from the table dropping a few coins on it and tucking his newspaper under his arm walked casually away.

He was a man with time on his hands and nowhere particular to be. As it turned out I also had the morning off and so followed him at a discreet distance until he turned up a hill I knew well. It was the hill I'd walked up every day for the last two months and yet I had never seen this man before. I was absolutely certain that here, not twenty yards ahead of me was Sir Donald Ingram, or Sir Phillip Upton as he now surely called himself. There was no way I could return to the hospital, but surely he knew I was working for him, how could he not if he was Sir Donald.

However, at the last moment the man in front of me turned abruptly and continued his stroll away from the hospital…but I had been so sure, so certain.

## Chapter Twenty-Five

Over the next few days, I'd returned to the cafe where I was sure I'd seen Ingram. I hadn't fully followed him on that first day as, as I have said I didn't know what I would have done if I'd stopped him and confronted him. I'd needed more time to think, to determine what the right thing, the moral thing was to do. I didn't want to kill him but thought that he would escape justice otherwise, but all I had done by hesitating was make no decision and let him slip through my fingers. What if I never saw him again? What if Sir Phillip was not Ingram? But what if he was? What would I do either way? The only way he would ever face justice for what he'd done for so long in England was if he were back in England. Here he was safe and he knew that.

I perhaps shouldn't have been surprised a few weeks later, after I'd seen the man I believed was Ingram, when I was called in to see Stanwick.

"Ah Weston, good of you to come and see me" the little man said
"And good morning to you as well Mr Stanwick, is everything alright?"
"Why yes, yes it is, please take a seat" I knew I was in trouble "Mr Weston, I hope you have enjoyed your time at St Francis?"
"Oh yes, definitely - it's a pleasure working here. The clients I see…"
"Patients…"
"Well - the people I see are troubled obviously, but there is usually a light at the end of their particular tunnels"
"Well that's good then…now Mr Weston…we have unfortunately, to let you go - or rather inform you that we will not be resuming your contract when it expires"
"Next week? You're sacking me?"
"Yes, next week, and no, we are not sacking you, that's such a harsh term. No. we are offering you alternative opportunities…elsewhere"
"And may I ask why Mr Stanwick? Have I done something wrong, or upset you, or someone else in some way?"
"No, not at all. We're just changing our business strategy that's all"

"I don't understand. What does that mean"
"We are going in a different direction"
"Which means..?"
"Which means we will not be renewing your contract when it expires - we will of course pay you to the end of the month, and provide you with a reference"
"Very gracious of you I'm sure. However, I would like to speak to Sir Phillip please. I would like to discuss this matter with him, if that would be possible?"
"That will not be possible I'm afraid"
"And why is that please?"
"He is currently abroad"
"Then may I have an address and I will write to him"
"Certainly. I will post it to you"
"I will wait thank you"

And that was that. I no longer worked at St Francis, or rather I did for the time being, but only until the end of next week. I immediately cancelled all my next week's appointments - the people I was due to see would survive until St Francis employed someone else. And, more importantly, by standing my ground Stanwick had furnished me with an address - an English address.

Could it be that simple? Was he giving me Upton's and therefore Ingram's English address?

I returned to the boarding house and told Laura what had happened - the man I'd seen at the cafe a few weeks ago and now my termination of employment. My own thought was that Stanwick only gave me the address in England so readily as he believed I wouldn't go there, that I wouldn't follow Phillip Upton - the man I thought was Ingram back across the ocean - after all I had no job there and no house either. Perhaps he thought I would just write to him and await a fuller explanation from the hospital owner. Before we crossed back over the Atlantic I needed to be sure, but I didn't know anyone left at the Spellbrook well enough to ask them to confirm my suspicions for me, and so I hesitated.

Laura however was adamant, saying that we should return to England immediately. Whilst initially she'd been keen to come to America I think perhaps she'd become disheartened by not finding Ingram in two years. She was also not happy that I hadn't told her about my possible sighting of him at the cafe and so we purchased tickets aboard the first ship sailing back to England.

I felt we needed to confirm things before confronting Ingram and I spent most of the long journey trying to convince Laura to wait, to make certain before doing anything rash.

When we got back to England several weeks later I still felt it best not to immediately go to Upton's house to confront him, and so I rented office space to continue my practice as a psychologist whilst I tried to confirm who he was in any way I could. I hoped that my English clients would be as verbally expansive, and as wealthy, as those I'd helped in America. I also wanted to speak to the police again and encourage them that they needed to deal with Ingram but Laura wanted to act as soon as possible. I don't think she trusted the police to be any more positive than they had been before and it became almost an obsession for her, poring over local papers in the hope of seeing a picture of Phillip Upton.

Over the next couple of months my clientele steadily built up and ranged from anxious and neurotic men and women who felt that the world would end if they couldn't balance a monthly budget during these difficult times; to people who felt they just 'had' to be introduced to the 'right' people in society or die trying.

There were also many parents who sent their children to see me when they felt they could no longer control them, or they were 'going off the rails' as the current expression was. In most cases there was nothing wrong with the 'child', most of whom were physically grown adults in their own right.

  I didn't mind which type of client I saw as the money people were prepared to pay allowed us to live a quite comfortable lifestyle, but I had recently been sent a letter which intrigued me. It requested an appointment for someone just called 'Albert', and the sender promised me a significant sum of money if I saw him, with more to follow if his 'condition' was diagnosed within the month.

  This was not possible and I thought I'd probably end up turning them away. I was not for hire after all and there was nothing that would make me change my mind or my principles.

Absolutely nothing.

## *Chapter Twenty-Six*

"Please, do come in and take a seat" I said as I held the door open.
"Sir" the man said
"I'm sorry?"
"Sir. You will kindly address me as Sir, or Your Lordship. During these meetings, you will at all times defer to my status. Do I make myself clear?"
"I understand you certainly, but what *you* perhaps fail to understand is that your father asked me to help you, and to help you I will need to get to know you. I am not a servant, I am not beneath you, either socially, or professionally, so what you need to understand is that here, in this safe space, there is no rank, no social structure and no need or want for social deference. I hope that I also make myself clear? And they are not meetings, they are sessions, therapy sessions"
"If you are to help me Doctor…"
"Mr"
"Really? Not even a proper doctor?"
"Oh, I am a proper doctor, but I call myself Mr, as you may, if you wish, Albert"

"If you are to help me…Mr Weston, then please know this. I only come here because my father is an extremely wealthy man and I will inherit that wealth when he dies. And I therefore am somewhat hamstrung if you follow me? "
"Oh? You believe he will die before you then?"
"Yes. Why would he not?"
"Spite? Stubbornness? I don't know I've never actually met the man, Albert."

This brought a slight smile from my prospective client which I thought was a small step forward for us both.

"Is he a difficult man - your father?" I enquired
"Difficult? That is too simple a word for my father Mr Weston, he is intolerable, insufferable, lost in his own generation and full of his own self-importance" Albert replied, and gave me a clue as to where he no doubt got some of his personality from

"Thomas" I said "Please call me Thomas"
"Not yet. I don't know you…perhaps next time"
"That's progress then, if you consider there may be a next time. So, would you like a seat? If you're staying obviously"

Albert, the son of the Duke of Brunswick then fully entered my office, took off his hat and gloves and having momentarily looked at me, perhaps to take them from him, thought otherwise and placed them on his lap as he sat in the chair opposite mine.

"No couch Mr Weston, nowhere to recline and tell you all my woes?"
"Couch, Albert?"
"Well, isn't that how this works?"
"What works? You haven't said anything yet. How do we know if anything works?"
"How long does this take…how many 'sessions' must I attend?"
" For what? "
" To be cured, to be…better? "
"Oh, do you think you are ill then Albert?"
" No. Certainly not. There is nothing wrong with me. As I have said I have been forced to come here, due to circumstances beyond my control"

I stood and reopened the recently closed door

"Then by all means, please leave"
"What?"

" Please leave. I want no man to say I have imprisoned him, held him against his will. If you don't want to be here, then by all means go. I only help clients who want to be here, and accept that need - that at least is in your control"

"Very well Mr Weston as you wish, and I am not your client. I do not wish to be here, my father made me come here, so I will wish you a good day" at which the man stood and made a very slow show of putting on his gloves and hat.

"Very well Lord Brunswick. Good day"

"You called me Albert not two minutes ago and now you address me by my title?"

"Ah, that is because you are no longer my client, Sir" I said, still holding the door.

## *Chapter Twenty-Seven*

A few days later I had just seen my last client of the day off the premises when there was a knock on my office door.

I wasn't expecting anyone and so didn't hurry to put the lid back on my fountain pen but waited a few moments to see if they would knock again.

Another knock duly came, this time more insistent, almost impatient, it was the knock of someone who was used to having doors opened for them, not closed to them.

I rose from my desk and as I walked towards it I think I already knew who would be on the other side of the door. I had been expecting this particular client in-waiting to return - he really had no choice and I think he knew it.

"Ah, Lord Brunswick, what a pleasant surprise, and what brings you to my doorstep, minus an appointment?"

"Appointment? Appointment Weston? You still know who I am don't you? My peerage hasn't disappeared since we last met has it? Now please, out of my way" the titled and entitled individual snarled as he pushed past me and strode into my office.

Had it been any other person I probably would have made an issue of the situation but I wasn't doing anything that evening and to be honest I needed the money that Albert's father would pay me, so I bore the intrusion.

"Please, Lord Brunswick, do come in, make yourself at home. Will you be staying, or shall I wait by the door again today?"
"Don't be an ass Weston. Shut the door. I am a busy man"
"And I am honoured that you spend some of your precious time with me Sir. How can I
help you..?"
"Albert - please call me Albert. I feel, having reviewed the circumstances, we may have started off on the wrong foot. There may have been words spoken, which in hindsight…"
"Shall we get started instead? There really isn't any need to apologise"

"Oh. I was not apologising, I don't apologise. I haven't done anything wrong, well nothing that concerns you"

"Ah. I see…well, we'll see shall we? Let's start with the easiest question although it is often thought of as the hardest…"

"Why am I here?"

"Precisely"

"No. I'm asking you. Why am I here Weston…sorry, Mr Weston, what can you do for me?"

"I think you can call me Thomas, if you're comfortable with that. I think it would put you more at ease in what must be a difficult situation for someone of your…your…for you, Albert, but please don't worry. It doesn't have to be difficult, or awkward. Nothing said here will be repeated to a living soul"

"Not even my father?"

"Especially not your father"

"Thank Christ for that Weston, I mean Thomas. Thank you for that. Shall I…?" he rolled his hand like he was starting a vehicle

"Please do - in your own time"

"I need you to declare me mad"

"Oh? Do you mean clinically insane, or just a little bit, it is thought that there are varying degrees of madness, which one would be most convenient for you Albert"

"Look, I know it sounds odd, a chap coming in here asking such a thing, but I have my reasons. Can you do it, will you?"

"I'm sure you do, but no and no"

"My father is paying you for my meetings with you"

"For your sessions, yes, although like a lot of the rich the service comes first and the payment is promised to follow"

"My father is good for the money, surely you know that? And God alone knows he spent enough of it on my brother - he can spend a little on me"

"Oh yes, I'm sure, it's just that it would be good to have a …what is it called?"

"An advance?" And with that Albert reached into his coat, pulled out his wallet and removed a folded bundle of banknotes. Laying them temptingly in front of me he said

"There, an advance. So, will you do it?"

"Albert. It's not that simple. No one is declared mad in a few days. What's happened? Why is there this urgency, what have you done?"

"Why must I have done something Weston? Surely you either will or will not do as I ask"

"Very well. Given those choices. I will not"
"Are you sure? When you have heard my tale you will understand my reasons. I also have come to you, specifically you, for a reason. I felt you would be most likely to help me"
"Oh really? Then by all means tell me your reasons, but that's not what I am here for, a quick fix or a qualified signature on a slip of paper for your convenience. Treatment takes a long time, months, sometimes years"
"I don't have years. No-one does. If I am discovered I may not have weeks let alone months"
"Then speak quickly Sir - tell me your tale".

## *Chapter Twenty-Eight*

Albert, the second son of the Duke of Brunswick then paused, took out a cigarette case, offered me one from it, which I declined, then lit his own and leaned forward, hands on his knees.

"Weston, I need to tell you a story, but it is not a happy one, and it is therefore very difficult for me to tell it"
"Take your time Albert, there is no hurry"
"I will tell you this tale but you cannot act on it, you must not act on it, for it will destroy your world if you do"
"Albert, I think there is little you can tell me that would have such an effect I assure you, and in any event I'm bound by the rules of confidentiality, nothing said here can be repeated to anyone without your permission. There are a few minor exceptions, criminal offences and so on, but please do continue"
"Ah. When you say criminal offences, which ones were you meaning exactly?"

"Oh. Please, don't worry, the major criminal offences - murder, robbery and so on, nothing for you to worry about. Please continue"
"I don't think I should Thomas"
"Albert please tell me your tale"

Albert then lit another cigarette, and smoked it fully down to the filter without saying a word to me. His whole body shook as he sobbed in between smoking. I couldn't believe this was the same man who'd pushed his way past me in such a lofty and cavalier fashion, seemingly only moments before. I looked at the clock on the wall and saw that although Albert had been in my office for nearly half an hour, I still couldn't get him to talk about what clearly troubled him so much, but once he started talking there was no stopping him.

"I have done terrible things; I have helped someone who did terrible things. Let me go back, let me start at the beginning. I had a brother - Edmund, he was the first son of a Duke and so he should have continued the line, but he was a deaf mute, an embarrassment to the family and so my father arranged for him to be housed at a hospital for the rest of his life. I know, this sounds awful but he was looked after well, treated with dignity and wanted for nothing, it was a good hospital.

The family however disowned him and claimed he had died in a fall; they even held a funeral for him. Things were good for Edmund though, all things considered, he had been placed at the Mountfield, do you know it?"

"I do, yes. It closed down a few years ago"

"Yes, and that was the issue. When it closed Edmund and many other people like him had to be rehoused. He was obviously placed there under an assumed name but eventually I found that he had been moved to…"

"The Spellbrook"

"The Spellbrook, yes, where conditions were, shall we say, not good"

"Awful in fact"

"Yes, awful. I continued to visit him, as I had when he was at The Mountfield, but found that his condition was deteriorating and I pleaded with my father to move him but he would not. He told me that he was happy to pay for Edmund to be there, out of the way but he would not move him - his own flesh and blood, and I was powerless. I don't have my own money and I am at the behest of my father, all I could do was shame him, and were I to do so I would lose my inheritance and be of no good to Edmund anyway.

Things continued getting worse for Edmund but there was one person at the Spellbrook who helped him, a nurse I believe, called Elizabeth, I think she was a nurse, and she communicated with him, via a chalkboard no less, and he told her who he was. At first I don't think she believed him but eventually he convinced her and she made him as comfortable as he could be in those terrible conditions, I can only imagine.
And then one day when I went to visit him he was not there, he had simply vanished, and they told me had died, and already been buried. But Elizabeth, she told me what had actually happened. She told me that one night some people took Edmund away and returned him some hours later. She told me that his head was bandaged and that when she looked he…he had no eyes! My God, if I could have found those people then I would have shot them on the spot, he was defenceless and in a supposedly safe place"

"But Albert, tell me, you didn't kill them, these monsters, did you?"

"You don't seem surprised by what I've told you Thomas? You don't seem shocked by the tale I've told you so far?"

"I was, I am aware of the awful things that went on at The Spellbrook, where I myself used to work. I reported them to the board and when I found out that it was my colleagues who were operating on the long-term patients I reported it to the authorities"

"And what did they do?"

"Nothing. They did absolutely nothing"

"Then maybe these people deserved what happened to them?

"What do you mean Albert, what happened to them? What do you know" I obviously had my own tale to tell regarding these men, but not yet, I wanted to know what Albert knew.

"I am coming to that. I said to Elizabeth that I would help her any time she needed my help. She had been so kind, so considerate with my brother and been with him when he died I felt I owed her, and I told her she only had to ask…but Thomas…what she asked… I couldn't have imagined anything so awful, so barbaric as what she asked me to be a part of"

"Tell me Albert, what was it? Who was this woman? Where is she now, do you know?"

"No. I do not, and I fear she has not finished what she started. She said there were others … "

"I think two others"

"Yes. But one of them was…"

" Albert, I need to be honest with you. I was arrested for what this woman did, what …"

"I helped her do"

"Indeed"

"Thomas, I did not know, I swear. I am so sorry"

"No need to be sorry, Albert, how could you have known? Now please continue"

"Well, you know the rest, you know what happened to these men, these surgeons, but I was there, and I helped her, I held them down while she…and I think my father knows I was there - his man - his aide saw me, with the woman, and no doubt he told my father"

"What makes you think your father knows, and even if he did…"

" He has sent me to you, to declare me insane, and when you have he will speak to the police, make this go away. So, you see, I need your help."

## *Chapter Twenty-Nine*

I knew I must help Albert - his was a sorry story indeed, but in my new found profession I couldn't just declare him insane to avoid justice. Insanity is not a thing that suddenly comes upon you, it isn't something you don't have one day and do the next.

I couldn't imagine the agony Albert had felt when his brother had died as he had. I was risking everything to help Albert and it troubled me that he had come, specifically to me - I was not the right person to help him, I was barely qualified in this area of medicine.

As I have said, many of my patients - clients now, were just looking for someone to listen to their troubles, an impartial ear to offer ideas and an independent thought of how to remedy their own particular situation, but Albert? His situation was dire - if word got out then he would surely hang, and even if he didn't the reputational damage to his family would be incalculable, and I had the feeling that his father would not allow that.

What struck me most though was that throughout all his terrible tale Albert had mentioned the woman, whom he called Elizabeth, but not what had happened to her. I could not imagine a woman doing the things he had spoken of; no woman could possibly do such horrific things and live with herself - what sort of monster would they be if they could?

I was lost in thought when Albert entered my office, and without introduction he said

"Thomas, I have some papers, which explain a situation, though not mine, but someone's who was close to me, and they may be of use to you?"
" What are they, Albert? What papers? " I asked him
"Read them Thomas, and see if they can be of use, I will of course pay you for your time - or rather my father will."

Albert passed me a file of papers some of which were seemingly quite old and as I looked through them I realised that they could very well help him in his current position, but they would need a little tailoring to suit his needs.

"This is your brother's medical record? "
"Indeed"
"How have you come by this Albert?"
"It is better that you do not know Thomas. Just accept that I have a lot of friends in a lot of places"

I didn't doubt that for one moment, but I also knew that if I did anything with these records and it was discovered, I would not only be struck off ever being any sort of doctor again, I would most likely go to prison, and I wouldn't risk that for anything, or anyone, let alone a man I'd only just met.

The door opened and Laura entered

"Oh, I'm sorry Thomas, I didn't know you had company"
"Good morning Madam, please excuse me attending unannounced, I will not take up much more of your husband's time"
"Not at all Your Lordship, that's quite alright, I've just brought the post, that's all. It's good to see you again" Laura said as she left the room and shortly afterwards so did Albert.

So, my wife and Albert knew each other? I could presume what I liked about many things but I didn't want to presume anything about Laura, I had to know the truth.

## *Chapter Thirty*

I found Laura in our bedroom, sitting, attending to some tapestry, a common way I think she found to calm herself, perhaps a throwback to when she had been at The Spellbrook.

      Whilst she had told me some things about her stays at the hospital I knew she had not been totally honest with me, but what I was thinking now was inconceivable. Had she been in the hospital at the same time as this nurse Elizabeth? Had she known the woman Albert claimed had murdered three people? My heart went out to her, and though she was calm at the moment I knew what I was to ask her would upset her terribly. I sat beside her and took the tapestry from her hands, holding them in mine. I took a deep breath and began

"Laura we need to talk, please"
"About what my love?"
" I have as you know just had Lord Brunswick in my office.
"Yes Thomas"
"And you seem to know him? "

"Yes Thomas, I do know him. I have known him for some time, well for a few years, but not closely"

Was this the thing I had dreaded for so long, had my wife been unfaithful to me with Albert? I had to know

"I need to know my love, how closely?"

" What is it you are asking me Thomas?"

"How closely do you know Albert?"

"What has he told you Thomas?" She looked straight at me.

"Nothing, Laura, nothing. I am asking you. How do you know Lord Brunswick?"

" He used to visit his brother when he was at the hospital "

" His brother…Edmund? "

" Yes, Edmund. Did he tell you about him? "

"A little yes…did you know Edmund?" I feared the answer

" Yes, I knew him, as far as anyone could know such a wretched soul. I helped him like anyone would…"

"Tell me more about Edmund please, for my own sanity"

"I helped him, that is all. He was deaf, and he couldn't speak, but we communicated well enough though. We used a chalkboard and he had quite a wide vocabulary. I helped him through his day and made him as comfortable as he could be at night…but then they came…in the night and took him away. He had the most beautiful eyes, so soulful…and they took them from him Thomas - they took his eyes! When they brought him back I knew he would die - can you imagine the rage I felt, myself strapped to the bed and all the while this poor man making no sound, no sound at all - but inside screaming in agony, and I could do nothing at all for him to ease his suffering. All I could do was talk to him, telling him he was not alone - but he couldn't hear me, as he died he had no one - I couldn't help him, and in the morning he was gone. Taken away and no doubt buried with all the others"

" You helped him as much as you could, that is all anyone could have done? "

"Yes. As anyone would"

"...Like a nurse would?"

" Well yes, I suppose so, yes, like a nurse would, I suppose I was a sort of nurse to him, and others, when I could be…when I wasn't strapped to a bed"

"And was that often?"

" Quite often during the day, yes, and always at night. I really shouldn't have been there. I've told you that my parents, if you can call them that, put me at…at that place, not for my own good as they would claim, but for theirs, for their…standing - they didn't want the embarrassment. Whenever I became unruly, and was too much for them, they sent me away"

"But I looked for you…"

"Looked for me?"

"In the records"

"Why? Why would you do that? What did you hope to find?"

"Find? I hoped to find you Laura. When you'd gone I hoped to find you, and talk to you…and save you. I never had the courage, when I first saw you…and then you weren't there"

"No. My parents took me back, that was when Eloise was born - at their house. I was 'cousin Laura' and my husband was 'abroad on business' until he 'died'

"Yes. Tell me about your husband, your first husband"

"Oh Thomas. You are such a trusting man…"

"What? Why do you say that? What do you mean?"

"There was no husband Thomas, there was only…a man"

"I know, I know. We have all fallen to temptation sometimes, and I've forgiven you my love, that's in the past"
"What? Forgiven me? There is nothing you need to forgive me for! I did nothing wrong, not then. Thomas…a man forced his way into my room at the Spellbrook, a man with all his wants and desires and…do I need to say it plainly?"
"What..? Forced himself upon you?"
"Yes Thomas, he did, and not only the once"
"So…Eloise..?"
"And Saul"
"What? Why did you go back there - surely your parents..? Surely the staff - the nurses..? How long did this go on?"
"Four years…four years until my white knight appeared"
"I..?"
"Yes Thomas, you. You saved me"
"This man…was it Albert? I will kill him! Coming here..!"
"No Thomas, it was not Albert"
"Then who - did you know him?"
"No. I did not know him then, but you did, for he was with you the first time I saw you"
"…Lawrence? You're saying that Lawrence forced himself upon you? No. That can't be Laura, that can't be, he wouldn't"

"It can, and he did Thomas. Why do you think I was so opposed to him coming to our house, staying with us, why do you think I spent so much time at my parent's house?"
"Are you telling me that the children were Lawrence's?"
"Yes Thomas"
"Both of them?"
"Yes Thomas, both of them"
"My God! I will kill him"
"No. You will not. I have already dealt with him"
"What? You've killed him? Laura?"
"No. I haven't killed him. His fate was much worse, much much worse"

I paused, my head in my hands…all this time I thought my wife was struggling mentally because of her parents' treatment of her, but that had been nothing compared to what she had suffered at the Spellbrook, while I was probably there, upstairs, or in my office whilst she was being…being…I couldn't bring myself to think of it. I would kill him; I would make it my one objective in life. I would hunt him down and make him suffer before he died at my hands.

Now I understood why he didn't want me talking to Laura when I first saw her, why he hadn't attended our wedding and why he tried to stay at our house when he thought she was at her mother's house - to avoid her. It made sense now.

"Where is Lawrence now, Laura?"
" I cannot say my love. Put him out of your mind. He will not bother us again"
"Cannot say, or will not? What did you do to him?
"It doesn't matter. He is gone from our lives"
"Did Ingram know about this? Did he let it happen?
"He knew. He sometimes came with Lawrence, and stood by the door…keeping guard, keeping watch - either him or one of the others"
"One of the others? Who? Who do you mean?"
"I didn't know their names, but they were doctors, they dressed like you, when you are working?"
"What? Are you sure? Are you absolutely certain?"
"I am certain Thomas"
"And these were the men who have been killed?"
"Yes"

I dreaded the answer to my next question, but I had to ask it.

"What name were you booked in at the Spellbrook under Laura?"
"I think you know Thomas. Are we finished?"

My wife, whom I knew less about than on the first day I had met her, got up, and walked from our room. As it turned out it was the last time I saw her, but I had always said I would lay down my life for her and so I would.

## *Chapter Thirty-One*

When he was arrested, for the second time, there were no protestations, no denials, just an acceptance that he was doing the right thing. Thomas had found out the truth and though he couldn't explain it, it all made sense to him, but he had needed to protect her, as he always had and so he remained silent throughout the interview.

When he'd realised what had happened Thomas accepted that he had been responsible for it all, and had taken the confessions Laura had given him, written by men while they still had their hands, and walked into the police station to admit his guilt.

*His* confession was readily accepted and whilst the body of Lawrence Jacobs was never found, those of Donald Ingram and his wife were, but four, five or six murders didn't really matter to him.

Thomas knew that he would hang, but so long as Laura was safe that was the only thing that mattered to him, and so he'd put her where she'd be the safest, back where he'd found her, back where perhaps she'd always truly belonged.

Thomas is brought down from the dock, he doesn't need to be escorted by jailers, nor be handcuffed, but he is. He will not try to run, for he has nowhere to go and no one to run to.

His fate wasn't even decided by a jury of his peers, he hadn't needed them to find him guilty, he'd known of his guilt for some time and willingly pleaded to it. Whoever did what and to whom, it didn't matter, it all came back to him, it was because of his actions, or lack of them that they caused the events to unfurl as they did; and he was willing to hang for it.

Thomas now sits in his cell and waits, will she come he wonders? He'd had Albert put her in the safest place he could think of, as part of their deal, and to try and stop *her* being at the court. But even if she came now she would be too late, there would be nothing she could do now.

His wife is safe and that is all that mattered, she is resting again. She has had no life of her own and deserves at least that now surely?

He *has* had a life. He'd had a good career; he'd enjoyed being what he'd been and he'd helped a great number of people for many years.

He'd had a wife and two children and had loved them dearly and now it was her turn. She deserved to be free and enjoy the things that he had and he was prepared to sacrifice everything, including his life for her.

## *Chapter Thirty-Two*

Three weeks later

The man sits and waits for the 'expert' to come to see him, to talk to him and to try to unravel his mind.

The expert chosen by the hospital is not one the man knows or has even seen before, but he looks forward to seeing him anyway as he doesn't get many visitors.

The expert walks into the room and takes a seat opposite the man. He crosses his legs as he unbuttons his jacket and makes himself comfortable, this may be a long session he thinks. It won't be easy; it won't be straightforward and it probably won't make sense to him though no doubt it will to the man he has come to speak to.

The expert takes out his pen and turns over a blank page in a new notebook. There's really no need to make such a show, surely the man knows the whole notebook is blank and unless he says anything spectacularly revealing the report is already written, the blank page is just to doodle on, when he's bored.

And so it begins, the man is brought back to the present, wherever he was in his mind forgotten, brought back to the here and now, to face up to today's reality, and explain if he can, why he did what he did.

The expert begins.

"So, Mr Weston, Thomas, can I call you Thomas?"
" Yes, please do "
" I am Leonard Abernathy. I am a doctor, the same as you, but in a different field"
"And how shall I address you Doctor Abernathy?"
"Doctor Abernathy seems as good a way as any I would have thought?"
" Very well, would you prefer to call me Doctor Weston then? Since I still hold that title also? Or Mr Weston, as I am still a surgeon, at least until next Thursday"
"Ah, I see. Then Leonard it is, you can call me Leonard"
"A simple test, no? Did I pass? You're writing already I see"
"Thomas. I'm here to speak to you, with you, to try and work out why you did what you did? Do you understand?"

" You know I'm to be hung soon don't you Leonard? Next week, Thursday will be my last day on earth. Do you understand that? "

"I'm aware of it Thomas, though I don't profess to understand it and I certainly don't agree with it. Ending your life won't bring back those you killed, it won't bring any peace to the deceased's relatives. But you gave no explanation to the court. You pleaded guilty to six counts of murder, without ever saying why. Executing you will not help things, but your explanation may do, it may help those of us that remain to better understand"

"Oh, I like you Leonard. If only we'd met sooner, perhaps you could have persuaded the judge that there was no point executing me"

"I've been asked to speak with you to get an understanding of your mind, an insight into it if you will"

"But for what reason Leonard? What difference will it make what I say? I'm either clinically mad, or clinically sane. Either way it doesn't matter. Whatever happened, happened, as you say nothing done to me will change that and so what benefit will there be, for anyone to know why?"

" I think it's so that people can understand why such things happen, why…"

"Leonard...I will tell you what happened, and my own reasoning behind it, but I can't imagine it ever happening again. I really don't think me telling you what was happening in my mind when I did what I did will prevent others from killing, and from taking things into their own hands, do you?"

" No. Probably not, but I need to compile a report…for the court? "

"Your report is no doubt already written. The judge won't read it anyway, so what does it matter?"

" Tell me anyway Thomas. Tell me, and let's see what happens shall we? "

" I will talk to you, I will tell you the truth, if you will be truthful with me. Are we agreed on that Leonard? Will we be honest men today, just here, just now? "

"Yes. I'll be totally honest with you. Why would I be otherwise?"

" You don't know what I'll say so how can you say you'll be honest, but let's proceed, and see what happens"

"Please do"

"As you know I was married and we had two wonderful children, whoever they were, whoever fathered them, they were wonderful children and even if they weren't mine I loved them like they were. One hundred percent, absolutely, and without question, until they were murdered. My wife was unfaithful to me, more than once if Saul and Eloise were indeed not mine, and she was unfaithful with my lifelong friend. How would that make you feel Leonard? How would you respond to that knowledge?"

" I don't know Thomas, I can't imagine"

"Then please try. Whilst I speak, try and imagine what you would have done"

"I will, but please, continue"

" My colleagues practiced their craft on mentally ill people, hundreds of them, most times without anaesthetic and left them to die in subhuman conditions below ground in the dark, their wounds gaping and becoming infected, leaving them to suffer and die horribly. And why did my employers do this Leonard? Not for experimental progress, not to advance medical science and to learn from their findings - that I could have almost understood, no, they did it for money, because of greed"

"If that was true why didn't you try and stop it? Why didn't you let the authorities know?"

'I did, but they wouldn't listen. The main perpetrator was a member of an elite club, and those who paid him to perform operations on their loved ones didn't care where the replacement organs came from, so long as they came. Ingram was a monster without doubt, but he was also so far ahead of his time. He carried out transplants that saved lives, important lives he would say if you knew his clientele, but at what cost? He would say none at all, but, as a doctor - a life is a life. It matters not if the mind has gone, that person still has as much a right to life as anyone else. People like Ingram, and there are many, are not Gods, they cannot decide who lives and who dies, only God can decide that"

"And yet you killed? You decided who lived and who died, Thomas."

"No. I decided who died. There is a difference. What happened was that people suffered, but three of those people killed each other, I did not kill, Radcliffe, Whitfield or Mortenson"

"No, perhaps not, but you removed their hands and sewed them together! You sewed three people together - having removed their hands, they were sewn together by their wrists for Christ's sake Thomas! And you left them to die!"

" Do not become emotional Leonard. That is what happened to them, it's true. But these three people, and it would have been five if I'd found Jacobs and Ingram then, these three people acted as one body, don't you see? They moved together in the hospital, they remained close to one another and they closed ranks and acted as one when they needed to. It was...what's the word? "

"Ironic? Freudian? "

" Appropriate Leonard, it was appropriate - they were given what they wanted. They wanted to be together and so they were. What is more appropriate than that?

They couldn't act separately, or think for themselves so they were made into the one person they wished to be, nothing more than that"

"And you removed their tongues?"

" Yes. That's also true, their tongues were removed. They would have killed each other sooner if they could have spoken. They were made to suffer, like they made us and hundreds of others suffer. They killed those dear to me - our children, they caused my beloved Laura to become a living ghost, they had to suffer, but not just for me - it was never just about me"

"So, it was a rational act, as far as you were concerned Thomas - a proper thing to do?"

" They were surgeons, but each of them used their hands for evil work, not good, don't you see? They were given the gifts they were but used them against people, not for them. And so, their tools of their trade were removed as they were no longer qualified to use them. It made sense what happened to them."

" But why plead guilty to killing them if you did not do it. Who are you protecting Thomas, and why? "

"It doesn't matter Leonard. It is done. The court accepted my plea, and I will hang for what I've done. I allowed things to happen and I am ultimately responsible."

"And Sir Donald? And his wife?"

" Ah yes, Sir Donald. Well Mrs Ingram knew me and she could identify me so had to die, that's common sense. It was unfortunate that she was there at all, she wasn't expected to be there and she did pull a knife on me. All I did was defend myself Leonard"

"But you had broken into their home? You had come to kill Sir Donald? Defending yourself?"

"It was relatively painless for Mrs Ingram, the knife I took from her was extremely sharp, one long pull across the throat, that was all. And as I killed her Ingram had to watch, as he woke, can you imagine that? Not as awful as waking to smell your children burning to death, but still quite bad I would think"

"But you smashed his skull into a thousand pieces Thomas…?"

" And it would have been more if I'd had more time Leonard I assure you. I *had* broken into their house, I was given no admittance, but my intentions were noble when I stepped foot into that enormous mansion. What happened is known only to a small number of people and two of them are, unfortunately dead, though I take a different view, naturally. I had been prepared to just confront Ingram with the evidence I had amassed, but his wife…his wife pulled a knife on me and again, unfortunately what he'd done to us took over in my mind, I wanted to make him feel a little of what I felt when he killed my family and so…he swung a hammer at me, and I reacted, now he'll never truly suffer, not like I did, not like so many others did"

"But he suffered in that moment, he must have suffered greatly, do you not think?"

" Do you know who Edmund Stanley was, Leonard? "

"Edmund Stanley? No, I'm sorry, I don't know who he was"

" Edmund Stanley was a patient at Spellbrook. Edmund was incarcerated in mental institutions all his life Leonard - can you imagine? "

"No Thomas, I cannot. It must have been quite bad for him"

"Quite bad? Quite bad Leonard? Do you know why Edmund was placed in such institutions?"

" No. I don't Thomas, but I think you're going to tell me"

"Edmund was a deaf mute. That was his crime Leonard. He couldn't hear or speak; he couldn't read or write and so he was thought to be mentally ill. And therefore as no one took the time to try to communicate with him he was incarcerated, locked up with violent, mentally ill people - for years Leonard, for years, and all with his family's consent"

"Why do you mention him Thomas, specifically?"

"Because when Ingram's head was smashed to beyond pulp it was also for the Edmund Stanley's of this world, and there were hundreds of them. Ingram selected Edmund for an operation. He removed Edmund's eyes, Leonard, his eyes! This wretched soul had only his eyes left to help him through the world and Ingram took them from him.

He was going to transplant them for money into the head of some Dame or Lady, but it never materialised, her husband changed his mind. And so do you know what Ingram did with them? "

"...No"

"He kept them in a jar in his library"

"No! No! That cannot be true Thomas, how do you know this?"

" Because they were there when I entered his house and I took them with me when I left so they could be returned to Edmund"

"But you cannot transplant eyes - it's not possible"

" Ah no, I should have explained, I meant to bury them with Edmund. You see Leonard, having removed poor Edmund's eyes Sir Donald Ingram, knight of the realm, left him to bleed out underground, in a dank, rat-infested room. He did nothing to help the poor man and neither did his assistant on the day - Samuel Mortenson"

"Mortenson was one of the six you killed"

"No. I did not kill him, or the other surgeons. They killed each other, though I do not know how"

"How do you know Ingram did this?"

" Because Mortenson wrote a confession, listing the times he'd aided Ingram. His confession with the other two was seized when I was arrested, when I walked into the police station".

"And confessed to the murders"

"And confessed to the murders, Leonard, yes. And now I need you to do me a favour, if you can"

"Yes, of course. I understand you have no family and have had no visitors whilst you have been here Thomas?"

"That's correct. My favour is this - if you ever meet someone who truly needs your help, I want you to help them. Can you do that?"

"Certainly"

"Don't just say it, Leonard. You promised you'd be honest with me. If you can't, then don't say you will"

"Thomas. I promise you. If I see someone who truly needs my help then I will help them to the best of my abilities. Do you have anyone in mind?"

"No. As I say. I have no one. But I think you will know them when you see them."

Thomas Weston was hanged the following week as he said he would be. He never gave a full account of what had happened to bring him to the gallows and went to his grave, a silent man.

## *Chapter Thirty-Three*

Two years later

Elizabeth wakes from a wonderful dream, she was walking on a beach, with a man and two children. The sand between her toes was real, the sun on her face something she could actually feel.

But today's reality, like yesterday's and all the days before that, is that she is underground, always underground, so much so that she can smell the damp, decaying building all around her. She would prefer the smell of the ocean from her dream, but she doesn't have that choice, and hasn't for some years.

She lies still, trying not to wake those around her, especially the woman in the next bed who likes to scream, from first thing in the morning until she is sedated back into silence.

Elizabeth feels sorrow for these poor people, she does want to help them, in any way she can - like she used to help people, for many, like her are here against their will and with no real reason.

The door opens and a nurse enters. She approaches Elizabeth's bed and puts her finger to her lips.

"I have a surprise for you Elizabeth, but you must be quiet" she whispers

Elizabeth nods, she understands.

"If I undo your straps will you be good?" The nurse asks.

Again, Elizabeth nods. She has not spoken since she was put here this time, taken again from the world she loved and deposited underground.

"Very well, but you will need these" the nurse says and hands Elizabeth a pair of sunglasses.

She is going outside, into the light, into real, fresh air. Perhaps she will feel grass between her toes today, not warm sand admittedly, but better than nothing she thinks. This nurse has often taken her outside, perhaps she recognises her from before, perhaps there is a kinship between them. Elizabeth has never been a cause for concern for the staff here, at The Spellbrook, never punched or bitten a nurse, like many have, and so she goes quietly, placing the sunglasses firmly on her beautiful face.

Elizabeth follows the nurse along the corridor, her keys jangling by her side, through gate after gate, each heavier than the last until she sees it, just a sliver at first, just a small shaft of light - outside light. Elizabeth hopes it will not be too much for her, like it was the last time. She follows the nurse through the last door, and there, there is the blessed light, air, grass, the outside world!

    Elizabeth stands for a moment just outside the door, and even though the sunglasses protect her from the worst, or best of the sun, she shields her eyes with both hands and mouths "thank you" to the nurse, who smiles and beckons her to sit with her on a nearby bench.

"Come Elizabeth, sit for a moment, I have things I need to tell you"

Elizabeth does as she is told, it's better that way, there is less pain that way. Some of the other nurses like to inflict pain on Elizabeth, perhaps they remember her from before. Perhaps they enjoy their power over her again, but this nurse, this nurse is different, she cares, and has a friendly face, she would never do harm Elizabeth feels, and so she sits, and waits.

"Elizabeth" the nurse starts gently. "What do you remember? From before? From before you were brought here?"

The nurse passes Elizabeth a glass of water and tells her to take her time. She knows that her patient *can* talk, but feels that she chooses not to.

"I remember a man, he was kind, he had soft hands, perhaps he worked with them?" Elizabeth pauses and tries to remember.

"Go on, Elizabeth. What else do you remember?" the nurse asks

"I cannot remember anything else; it is very vague; it has been too long"

"You have been here a long time; do you remember the first time you were here?"

" The first time? "

"Yes. You were perhaps sixteen? You had come to us as your parents could not help you. Do you remember?"

" I was in America. I remember America"

"Yes. But that was later, much later. But often…you came to us. But you haven't always been here. Think of here as somewhere you come for a rest, in troubled times"

"But I am strapped to a bed at night, people scream and shout and say all kinds of murderous things all the time - how can I rest here? "

"I know. It's not ideal, but there are a lot of troubled people here, a lot of tortured souls that maybe are past help, but we try to care for them, and you - we care for you as best we can, you know that don't you? "

"Yes, I know you do what you can. But tell me, who am I? What is my name"

"We call you Elizabeth. When your parents put you here, many years ago, they told us you were called Laura, but you seemed to react badly to that name and so we called you Elizabeth, and we have called you that ever since. But you have had a good life - and a lot of it outside these walls, try to remember"

"How long have I been here? I can't remember much of another life - a different life. Was I married? Did I have children? Why can I not remember?"

" You *were* married Elizabeth, to Thomas - he was a doctor here once - perhaps he was your man with soft hands. Now, there is someone I want you to meet. He is a doctor too Elizabeth, and he wants to help you. Will you speak with him, here in the gardens?"

## *Chapter Thirty-Four*

The woman sits and waits for the 'expert' to come to see her, to talk to her and to try to unravel her mind, though that's probably a lost cause, as she's not been able to do that herself, so why would someone else be able to.

The expert chosen by the hospital is not one the woman knows or has even seen before, but she looks forward to seeing him anyway, she doesn't get many visitors, and it will pass the time she thinks.

The expert walks towards her and takes a seat beside the woman. He crosses his legs as he unbuttons his jacket and makes himself comfortable, this may be a long session he thinks. It won't be easy, it won't be straightforward and it probably won't make any sense to him though no doubt it will to the woman he has come to speak to, if she will speak to him, he understands that she has hardly spoken a word since she was brought to the hospital where she now resides.

The expert takes out his pen and turns over a new page in a new notebook, though this time the whole notebook is not totally blank, but there aren't many details about this subject, as not much is known about her.

And so it begins, the woman is brought back to the present, wherever she was in her mind forgotten, brought back to the here and now, to engage with today's reality, and be asked to explain if she can, why she is here. Though she knows that nothing she says will change her position.

The expert begins.

"Good morning, Elizabeth…may I call you that?"
"If you wish" the woman says, her voice is cracked and it seems an enormous effort for her to speak.
"I am Doctor Leonard Abernathy and I am the resident psychiatrist here at The Spellbrook"

The woman nods, it's easier to do that than speak.

"Do you know what a psychiatrist is Elizabeth?"

She nods again.

"I know it is hard for you to speak, I understand that you have been here at The Spellbrook for nearly three years and haven't said very much to anyone"

The woman shrugs, and doesn't respond as there doesn't seem to be a question in the man's statement.

"I also understand that no one actually knows who you are"

Another statement, another shrug.

"Can you tell me anything about yourself Elizabeth? We're trying to help people here to see what we can do for them, and to see if there is anything we can do to make their lives easier, better, more rewarding, if that's possible. Would that be possible for you, do you think?"

The woman takes a sip of the water from a glass on the table before her. She takes her time, there is no need to rush. She knows she is not going anywhere, and there is nothing that could make her life easier, nothing that could be rewarding for her.

Everything she ever had has gone, most of it went many years ago. She begins to speak but it's hard for her, where does she start, how does she tell her story?

She brushes a speck of lint from her dress, the cuffs neatly and expertly sewn by her own hand many years ago. She decides to start at the beginning.

"Dr Abernathy, Leonard. You can call me Elizabeth, though that isn't my name. It doesn't matter what my name is, I have no identity, no purpose, no meaning. I have, as you say, been here for at least two years, though you'll not find a record of me coming here. I've been attended to by staff who try their best. They're not trained to look after the likes of me and those I share these wards with. They are medically trained but most know next to nothing about the mind."

The woman pauses and takes another drink of water.

"I'm sure…" Abernathy says
"Now I'm speaking, you want to stop me Leonard?"
"No. I'm sorry, please go on"

"From the beginning I told the staff the truth, the real version of events that brought me here, but they wouldn't listen. They thought I was mad and treated me accordingly. I told them time and again that they were about to hang my husband for crimes he had not committed"

"Who was your husband Elizabeth…can I ask you that?"

"It doesn't matter. No one listened then, and he is no more. I will see him in another life when my time comes, if he will meet me. If he will forgive me"

"I am sure he will - what did he do…may I ask?"

"You met him once"

"Really? Where?"

"I don't know Leonard. I've been underground this time for nearly three years, don't forget, but I understand you interview those who are condemned to hang?"

"I've met so many people in the last three years, Elizabeth. I don't know who you mean"

"Thomas Weston. My husband was Thomas Weston"

"Oh my God…you are Laura, Laura Weston?"

"I am. Though no one believes me"

"But you died in America. Thomas told me that he left you there while he came back to England…to…do what he did"

"Well I am here am I not? Ask me anything about Thomas, let me convince you"

"Laura. I don't know what to ask you. I don't know what to say to you. Why are you here then? What did you do to end up here?"

"Thomas had me put here for my own safety. He believed that this was the best place for me…"

"While he killed others? While he…you know what he did don't you Laura?"

"Leonard, I know what he was hung for. For killing people who had killed others, for taking the law into his own hands. But he was wrongly convicted on many counts. You do know that don't you?"

"No I don't, Laura. He didn't defend himself at Court. He dismissed his barrister and pleaded guilty, and was hung for his crimes"

"And what he said was then just accepted. Even by you Leonard, an expert"

"But why would he say what he said if it were not true"

"Because he was about to hang. It didn't matter what he said then, nothing he said would have been believed. The story fit and so was accepted - someone so under pressure that he couldn't cope anymore and killed those who had wronged him. That was how it was portrayed, and that was what was believed"

"We must get you out of here Laura. Things have moved on - you should be released, you should be allowed to walk out of here, you've done nothing wrong"
"And where would I go? What would I do? Our house was burnt down and my family was killed"

"I will find you somewhere. I will find you accommodation. You are not insane Laura; you don't deserve to be incarcerated a moment longer. Now you must excuse me. I now have to see a wretched man - a poor soul who…well never mind - I will be back soon, hopefully with good news for you Laura".

Laura quietly followed Leonard back into the hospital, along the corridor and saw him sit next to the bed of a man covered in bandages. The patient does not speak. He would learn sign language to aid his communication with his limited underground world but it would do him no good. He was brought to The Spellbrook two years ago having suffered terrible burns to his face and hands, so bad that his tongue and hands had to be surgically removed.

He was then strapped down to the bed as even the sedation they gave him failed to fully numb the pain and he thrashed wildly for the first few days. Now all he does is lie still and think.

The sign above the man's bed says John Doe as no-one knows who he is - no one that is except Laura.

## *Epilogue*

A year later

As I walk towards my lodgings, I think that Leonard Abernathy has been honest, and true to his word - perhaps as a way of keeping his promise to Thomas - he has helped a person truly in need.

It's wonderful to be free again, to see the sky and breathe the fresh clean air. Having been underground as long as I was, in a room as small as it was, it tires me walking too far, but walk I must, I know that I have to keep walking - I've been locked up during the day and shackled to a bed at night, for so long that when I get the chance to walk I just have to. I may be seen by someone who knows who I actually am, and knows what I did and the thought of being taken off the street and put underground again or worse terrifies me, and so I walk, head down as quickly as I can from the factory where I am a seamstress, to my lodgings.

As Thomas probably told you he didn't have a bad childhood or a poor education, and neither did I, so I really have no excuse for what I did.

Thomas was a very intelligent man, but too trusting by far, too willing to believe everything he was told. He saved me from my own private hell and also of being operated on when my time came at The Spellbrook, by marrying me - we had had a courtship of sorts whilst I was incarcerated underground and often met in the gardens when a kindly nurse took pity on me from time to time.

He accepted my story that the two children he knew I had had were from a previous marriage and that my husband had died. And perhaps Thomas really hadn't known the truth of who had fathered Saul and Eloise before I told him, although it was not an affair I had had with Lawrence as I think he suspected.

There were people, sicker than those they preyed on, that availed themselves of whatever and whomever they desired, in the dark underground hell that I had called home for so long.

Lawrence, and the others…well, they had to die for what they did, but first they had to suffer. I saw those I loved burn to ashes before me and I defy anyone seeing that not to go insane.

So, now you know the truth. It was me who did it all, not poor Thomas, he did nothing wrong, how could he? He was a doctor, and he swore an oath, but I didn't. There was no Hippocrates on my conscience when I cut the hands from three evil men and sewed them together, leaving them to suffer and die.

It was me who set fire to Lawrence and left him outside the hospital, and he is now where he deserves to be, minus his hands and tongue obviously - he can lie there and suffer for all time as his punishment.

And my parents? - yes me as well - that was too good an opportunity to miss. Ingram would always look to cover up the fire as an accident, and so I used his reasoning after my children died in their sleep.

And it was me who didn't hesitate to slit the throat of Mrs Ingram, who knew exactly what her husband did and lived so finely on the proceeds of his evil deeds and never said a word.

But I must admit I enjoyed saving the best until last.

As Thomas has already told you it was for Edmund Stanley, and those like him. His surname was obviously Brunswick, and he was the first son of the Duke of Brunswick, locked up by his family, as I was, and left underground for years, until Ingram and his men selected him, and used him for their own ends, and I had made a promise to his brother Albert that if he helped me I would avenge Edmund's death.

So, it was me, not Thomas, who entered the Ingram's house as they slept and it was me who sat astride Sir Donald. And it was me who used his own hammer to smash his brains beyond oblivion, for it was his mind I wanted to destroy, not his body. He'd set up a hospital as a cover for his wicked practices, and had run it for years, allowing whoever was willing to pay enough to be a member of his club and do whatever they wanted to helpless people and all because of money.

And so, to answer my own question - yes, I think what I did was justified, don't you?

Printed in Great Britain
by Amazon